Herbert Byng Hall

The Adventures of a Bric-a-Brac Hunter

Herbert Byng Hall

The Adventures of a Bric-a-Brac Hunter

ISBN/EAN: 9783337341930

Printed in Europe, USA, Canada, Australia, Japan

Cover: Foto ©Andreas Hilbeck / pixelio.de

More available books at **www.hansebooks.com**

THE ADVENTURES

OF

A BRIC-A-BRAC HUNTER.

BY

MAJOR H. BYNG HALL,

AUTHOR OF "THE QUEEN'S MESSENGER."

LONDON:

TINSLEY BROTHERS, 18, CATHERINE ST., STRAND.

1868.

LONDON:
BRADBURY, EVANS, AND CO., PRINTERS, WHITEFRIARS.

PREFACE.

A PORTION of this work was published in the "Belgravia" Magazine. The limits and delay of a periodical, however, by no means permitted the author to enter fully on his subject. Moreover, his intentions were in some measure weakened.

In no manner does he presume to be a first-rate connoisseur as regards the ceramic art, which is scarcely to be obtained in the researches of a life. One science bears so closely on every other, that without a knowledge of all there can be no complete acquaintance with any.

His object is simply to give a slight sketch of his various hunting-grounds in search of bric-à-brac—a very simple pursuit—which has caused him untiring interest and delight; and thus, by offering the slight practical experience he has gained during foreign travel, he may cause amusement, if not instruction, to the many thousands who have similar tastes, when they visit the hunting-grounds where he has so frequently wandered.

H. BYNG HALL.

LUCERNE,
18th August, 1868.

CONTENTS.

THE ADVENTURES

OF

A BRIC-A-BRAC HUNTER.

QUEST I.

ON BRIC-A-BRAC IN GENERAL.

"Southey was right when he told his brother that if he would use his eyes on his travels, and in his own natural language describe truthfully all that he saw, he would be enabled to entertain the most educated reader, and charm the least."

"Art, like poetry, is addressed to the world at large."

IN a useful little work entitled *Les Eccentricités du Langage Français*, I find the word "Bric-à-brac" or "Bric-à-bracquer" explained thus:—"*revendeur de meubles et d'objets d'art.*" The celebrated Monsieur Pons, a remarkable collector of days lang syne—a romance of whose life has been so ably imagined and written by Balzac—continually uses the words bric-à-brac and bric-à-bracquer; the latter simply implying a collector, or one passionately devoted to works of art.

B

In plain English, the amiable and valuable
promoters of this refined pursuit are generally
alluded to as "curiosity-hunters;" but this denomination is, to my mind, a gross and uncourteous error,
inasmuch as works of art, of whatever nature, if they
be of any value, can scarcely be denominated
curiosities, although a curiosity may possibly be a
work of art. I own to a very unpleasant indignation
when asked to exhibit my humble collection as if it
were a Museum of Curiosities: while poor Monsieur
Pons was as jealous of his art-treasures as an ardent
lover of his mistress, and scarcely desired that any
eye save his own should behold them. Like Othello,
he would not "keep a corner of the thing he loved
for others' uses." In our day bric-à-brac shops
abound in all the capitals of Europe, as well as in
most large towns abroad and at home. These emporiums of art and virtu are commonly called
"curiosity-shops," because possibly it has been found
difficult to describe them more correctly. I deny,
however, *in toto* the accuracy of the term. A
Worcester or a Wedgwood vase, Sèvres, Dresden, or
Vienna cups, Capo di Monte or Chelsea groups, are
not curiosities, but, if good specimens, are works of

the most refined art ; though they may be found in
the so-called curiosity-shops. If these emporiums of
precious things are curiosity-shops, it certainly
follows that the Kensington Museum, the Musée de
Sèvres, the Vienna Museum—collections public or
private—should, in fact, all come under the same
denomination.

I confess I have as yet never been able clearly to
ascertain why certain individuals of varied tastes
and habits become as they advance in life the
collectors of china, old plate, manuscripts, auto-
graphs, pictures, and all those miscellaneous objects
of art or relics of past generations classed under the
comprehensive name of antiquities, apparently
without having any refined or ardent taste for the
rare and the beautiful. It matters little who they
are ; but it is a fact that there are nowadays thousands and tens of thousands of persons whose pre-
vailing passion is the collection of "bric-à-brac"—in
which comprehensive term I include all that is
precious and beautiful as well as mediocre in art,
whether pictures, porcelain, ivory or wood carving,
terra cotta, miniatures, jewelry, or plate. I can fully
understand that the man of wealth should be

anxious to adorn his home with works of rare art,
works to be looked on and admired by others, yet on
which individually he may scarcely care to gaze, and
of the real value of which he is in a great measure
ignorant. I can also fully understand that the
dealer in " bric-à-brac " should be desirous of obtaining a thorough practical knowledge of the value of
the goods which he barters, in order that he may
buy in a cheap market and sell in a dear one, till
eventually the love of art-possessions may so creep
into his heart that even his commercial soul may
suffer a pang at parting with some rare and precious
object; and I know that among the higher class of
dealers there are to be found men of varied attainments and great taste and knowledge. But I know
also that the Honourable Mrs. Bonheur, or my Lady
Lovecup, will very often invest a large amount in the
purchase of a Sèvres cup of that most lovely colour
termed "Rose du Barry," or of a Wedgwood vase of
the most elegant form and design, in order that
others may envy and admire; while to the fair and
aristocratic possessor herself the one is a mere cup,
the other simply a vase.

I believe my friend Mrs. Haggleton's taste for

collecting the plate of Queen Anne's era originated in the fact of her aunt having left her a teapot of that admirable period of the goldsmith's art in England. The teapot inspired an ardent desire to possess other articles in the same style. The lady mildly commenced with salt-spoons, and became in due course the proud owner of mustard-pots, salt-cellars, and one large piece of sideboard plate, which from the day she purchased it to that of her death every night faithfully accompanied her to her bedroom. My old bachelor friend Croker, again, began collecting Wedgwood ware because some one had told him he possessed a very fine specimen; while to my certain knowledge he was as ignorant of its value and exquisite design as his own footman could have been.

There are, however, far higher and more agreeable motives which lead the man of refined taste to become a real practical collector, whatever his position or means; and when that man is found who collects from pure devotion to art, he at once becomes a benefactor to the human race, as his object is to instruct and improve the artisan of our day, whether it be in furniture, lace, porcelain, jewelry, texture designs, or wood-carving.

It is an obvious fact that the art-genius of the day in which we live is turning to the past for its designs. We invent nothing that is new and beautiful, but we repeat much of the beautiful of past periods. Our jewellers owe their most elegant designs to Etruria and Greece. In domestic furniture we are reproducing the graceful forms of the French upholsterers who furnished the salons and boudoirs of Athenais de Montespan, the Pompadour, the Du Barry, and the luckless daughter of the Cæsars. And when we aspire to make our dinnertables elegant, we seek to imitate the delicate fragility of mediæval Venetian glass, embellished with designs copied from classic examplers. And the bric-à-brac shops of all the capitals of Europe are filled with lace, every design of which is a revival.

Now all these manifest features of industrial art are to be attributed to the collections of those who have dedicated their time and experience to the gathering together of various specimens of the art of past ages. The treasures of the Kensington Museum and those in Paris, Vienna, and elsewhere, which have lately been thrown open to the public, are of infinite practical utility. Yet I will venture to say that the individuals who collected these art-treasures commenced their pleasing labours in the first instance from the simple desire to gratify personal vanity, or with the less noble thirst of gain. Say nay who will, there is no greater pleasure to the collector than that of buying cheap and selling dear, even if money be no great object. Indeed, I have known more than one collector sell his whole collection for the mere pleasure of recommencing his researches for another, or to obtain some precious and unique relic, the possession of which shall elevate him above all vulgar connoisseurs. Depend upon it the collector is more or less the slave of vanity, although he may be also a man of taste. My experience tells me that there are people who claim as their own a rare Venetian glass, a noble Wedgwood vase, an exquisite Sèvres cup, or an elegant Dresden group, or any perfect or rare object of art, who would like to smash every one else's vase or group, as the Dutch tulip-grower would have crushed under his feet the rival bulb of a rare and precious flower, that it might bloom in no other garden than his own.

The amateur collector who wishes to indulge in a little traffic with his friends need not be ashamed of dabbling in the business of the bric-à-brac merchant. Very aristocratic individuals have dealt in such merchandise.   His Highness the Duke of Brunswick deals in diamonds ; and the Duc de Morny was a dealer in pictures, as was Marshal Soult before him. When once a man becomes a collector, he can hardly escape becoming a seller.

The Children of Israel have always been conspicuous dealers in the fine arts ; and the Rothschilds are well-known collectors of the finest art-treasures of the past.

Kings and queens, emperors and men of high degree, for centuries past have loved the ceramic art with no common passion ; while, by an assiduous cultivation of the same art, men of low birth and little education have raised themselves to honour and high estate.   Who that dwells with pleasure on the search for bric-à-brac has not perused the fascinating life of the poor potter Palissy ? What collector does not remember the struggles and triumphs of the noble-minded Wedgwood? What worshipper of art has not listened to anecdotes of Böttcher and De Blaquier?

The Chinese emperors by high rewards alone obtained the then unrivalled egg-shell china, since so gracefully imitated, and sold for so low a price. The Celestials testified their admiration of the inventor by enrolling the potter-martyr in the catalogue of deities.

The Duke of Urbino introduced the highly artistic, if not the graceful, majolica.

Henry II. and Diana de Poitiers gave the name to the varied beauties of Faience ; while that prince and his consort, Catherine de' Medicis, developed the genius of Palissy. Augustus the Strong, Maria Theresa, Frederick the Great, and other reigning princes of Germany founded and brought to perfection at their own expense the porcelain manufactories of their respective countries. Russia, where day by day the art is improving, and where it has indeed already obtained considerable celebrity, owes to Elizabeth and Catherine the Second its progress. In Italy royal patronage also nurtured the ceramic art.

Charles III.—whose memory be honoured for this single act—founded the unrivalled manufacture of Capo di Monte and Buen Retiro, to my taste the most interesting and refined of all ornamental china, not excepting Sèvres, which Pompadour's influence over Louis XV. helped to bring to its elegant perfection ; while the bewitching Jeanne Marie Vaubernier secured the lovely rose colour so well known and so highly esteemed among connoisseurs as Rose du Barry.

At home we have as high, if not higher, claims to the perfection of ceramic art. William, duke of Cumberland, supported the far-famed manufactures of Chelsea, while the name of Queen Charlotte added to Wedgwood's glory.

Men of all ages, all countries, all ranks have devoted themselves to the worship of this beautiful in art.

I have known a dignitary of the Church, a man of high attainments, a Christian in all the attributes of life, to go home from a sale with a bilious attack because he had failed to secure a group bearing the monogram of Carl Theodore, for which porcelain— and I fully sympathised with him—he had an intense liking. One of the keenest sportsmen of my acquaintance was as eager to obtain a Sèvres cup that he had been longing for as to kill his fox after an hour's run. Ay, and two of our bravest admirals, Nelson and Byng, were not only intense lovers of the ceramic art, but bric-à-brac hunters; in the families of each are retained valuable relics of their labours.

Seeing that the collection of rare and precious examples of art has now become a fashion as well as a passion, I venture to think that the friendly advice of a moderately experienced collector may be of some value; and with that belief I propose to tell my readers how for years, amid the varied pursuits of life, the search after bric-à-brac has afforded me days and hours of unalloyed pleasure, not altogether unaccompanied with profit, and always combined with great interest and instruction.

To the wholly ignorant amateur no book ever published, however valuable, interesting, or correct it may be, is of much avail; whether it be Braignart or any other, not excepting that most useful work to all collectors, the Catalogue of Bernal's Sale, published by Mr. Bohn, who is himself the owner of a most valuable and highly interesting collection of

varied porcelain and ancient pictures. If the bric-à-
brac hunter have not the eye for art combined with
refined taste, whether as regards ancient or modern
works, together with years of practical knowledge,
he is a mere child in the hands of the dealers; and
even when possessed of taste and experience he is
not unfrequently deceived. An extensive and correct
list of works is of great theoretical service to the
collector; but, alas, in the age in which we live, I
have yet to learn that there exists any article ever
produced by the inventive mind and hand of man
that cannot be in some measure—ofttimes admirably—imitated. I therefore venture to assert,
after long years of constant practice and study, that
practical knowledge, that instinctive appreciation of
perfection, which is the fruit of long experience, are
the only real and efficient guides by which the bric-
à-brac hunter may secure prizes in the markets of
the world. A Sèvres cup may be a Sèvres cup, and
worthless, save that it is Sèvres. There is Wedgwood and Wedgwood. Between two Dresden groups
there may be all the difference of the highest and
lowest art. A Carl-Theodore figure may bear clearly
developed the initials of Carl Theodore and the

Crown Elector of Palatine, a Berlin cup may be graced with the pencil of a Watteau, and yet the specimens may not be true, the porcelain may not be fine, the outline and execution may fall far short of that perfection which alone can satisfy the eye of the accomplished connoisseur. Again and again will the novice in these researches become the victim of his own ignorance, unless he avails himself of the taste and experience of some practised collector. How is he to distinguish hard paste from soft ? how resist the fascinations of modern Wedgwood, which, beautiful as it may be in its form and colour, lacks the keen and artistic outline of those never-dying productions of Wedgwood's own day ? Will the novice judge and estimate the merits and demerits of the Marcolini and the royal period of Dresden china ? No, believe me ; clever as he may consider himself, he will not.

Look at some of the old productions of Frankental and Carl Theodore. How striking in character, how lovely in design and execution ! what living figures produced in clay ! Gloat, if you be a connoisseur, on a Capo di Monte or Buen Retiro group, whose living grace and loveliness have scarcely been rivalled by

the sculptured art of Canova or Gibson.   What avails
it to tell you of the works so carefully produced, in
the words I have named to you?   If the passion for
such works of art exist not in your heart, second only
to the love of woman, you may seek for treasures in
vain ; and your researches will only obtain for their
result the merest everyday specimens, to be picked
up in the highways and byeways of every capital in
Europe.

Think me not presumptuous. *Moi, qui vous
parle*, am only a humble collector, and have been
frequently deceived, though the passion has reigned
for many a year in my breast, and is in a manner
hereditary.   For many years I have followed the
pursuit of a collector throughout the length and
breadth of Europe.   Alas, only in the most simple
and economical fashion.   But far removed as my
power of purchasing may be from that of a Rothschild, it has been my privilege to linger with admiring eyes and longing heart over some of the
finest specimens in Europe.   I have gloated, I have
longed, and then have flown from those treasures as
from typhus-fever, conscious of my inability to purchase the finest, and not caring to possess inferior

examples, or modern manufacture. But if my means are not large, my experience has been extensive; and as an official wanderer over the face of the earth, I have been enabled from time to time to peep into many a bric-à-brac shop in the various continental capitals, which others may never have had the chance of visiting. Thus have I made friends with many a choice specimen, erst the ornament of a palace, and have by good fortune secured some small treasures for the adornment of my cottage home. As I smoke my meditative cigar, and gaze with contemplative eyes upon those precious Sèvres cups and groups, which are to me as are his scalps to the Indian warrior, memory recalls many a quaint record of my wanderings and researches, which may be of value to those who may chance to follow in my footsteps in search of a bric-à-brac, and which may not altogether prove uninteresting to those who are comparatively indifferent to these ceramic pursuits. In my early boyhood, I confess for many a year to have imagined that all the fine specimens of china I looked on were the productions of the Chinese. I believed, in fact, that china was made in China, and in China only. But years passed on, and I found that, after all, that

which is termed Oriental china and Japan ware was
far less pleasing to my eye and taste than those
works of art which are purely European.

In Addison's day no aristocratic mansion was considered properly furnished without a vast quantity
of grotesque objects in china, or, as the ladies called
them, "loves of monsters." Oriental china was then
contraband; and I conclude that everything that
was contraband was fashionable. Many of these
"loves of monsters" may be had in the days we live
in; and I trust my readers may learn not to be
taken in by them, unless they chance to discover a
monster of pure "forget-me-not blue" of real an-
tiquity, and then both his mane and his tail are of
value. The colour must be that beautiful tint which
the French term *blue d'œil*, and which makes some
specimens of Sèvres invaluable.

And now, ere I ask my readers to walk with me
through many a high-street and bye-street of the
various capitals I have visited, and pass with me a
few hours in pure bric-à-brac hunting, I must own
to being an enthusiastic lover of art, whether that
art be that of the painter or the sculptor, or whether
it arise from the noble institutions of Sèvres, Dresden,

Chelsea, Derby, Frankental, Höchst, Capo di Monte, or Buen Retiro, from the never-dying elegance of Wedgwood, or the more recent talent of Minton. To my mind there can be no purer pleasure than this unaffected love of art, nor is there any taste more elevating in its influence on a man's nature; for I most fully believe that he who possesses this taste, and cultivates it, will soon turn his back on the grosser pleasures and frivolities of life. The higher order of art is, moreover, the constant handmaid of religion; and many of the great masterpieces which adorn the collections of Europe owe their origin to the inspirations of piety, and have been for centuries, and are still, powerful aids to meditation and devotion. Art has, and ever will have, a high and noble mission to fulfil.

That man, I think, is little to be envied who can look on works of art and go forth without being in some sense a better and a happier man ; if, at least, that we feel ourselves the better and the happier when our hearts are enlarged, as we sympathize with the joys and sorrows of our fellow-men.

I have not seldom been asked by those who have chanced to visit my cottage home—the windows of

which look on a small' but well-kept lawn, o'er-
shadowed by trees such as are rarely seen out of
England, and which lies within gun-shot of the
winding Thames—what possible delight I can have
in so small a room crammed with old china. It is
true, my treasures are generally admired; true, that
the specimens which during my travels I have
gathered together at trifling cost are coveted by
many; while the questions, "Are you not afraid
they will be broken? who do you get to dust them?
why not sell them?" and so forth, are asked with
unfailing sameness. The reply of my only and
motherless boy, if present, is as follows: "They are
papa's toys; he is keeping them for me." I should
be almost ashamed to confess *how much* pleasure
these fragile treasures afford me. For hours I sit
amidst my friends, pen or book in hand. That
group before me was purchased under particular
circumstances, and not only recalls to mind pleasant
days, but tells me much of the history of the country
whence it was obtained, and the era in which it was
produced. Who will venture to say that the lips of
a Pompadour or Du Barry may not have kissed those
small but exquisite Sèvres cups? Is not Wedgwood

paying me a morning visit with his friend Flaxman as I look on those vases? Do not the guns of Wellington's artillery sound in the distance as I contemplate that glorious group of Buen Retiro? And does not the Bay of Naples spread itself before me, and the towering peak of Vesuvius send forth its flames, as I handle that creamy china cup, with its exquisite painting of Capo di Monte? My Chelsea ware recalls the memory of Addison, who dated so many of his pleasantest essays from that locality. My Battersea reminds me of sceptical Jacobite Bolingbroke. At one moment I am at Florence, then at Vienna. For a few minutes I dwell in the Palatine, and thence take wing to Dresden. Now I touch my lips with the thin emerald-coloured glass of early Venice, then hold aloft the heavier but richer goblet of Bohemia.

Meanwhile I endeavour to create in the mind of that boy, whom love induces me to mention, and who calls these gems my toys! yet never breaks them as his own, that it is not the mere graceful work of art on which you look, whatever the pleasure, that is alone valuable, but the knowledge gained of the early art history of other countries, which adds to the ceramic collector's pleasure and instruction.

Moreover, it is pleasant to human nature to feel that you possess some work of art which is admired by those who have full knowledge of its beauties; but if this were all the merit of your researches, the reward would be light indeed.

From the earliest ages to the hour my pen traces these lines, the earth, which God has granted for the produce of man's sustenance, has also contributed to his pleasures; and science and art have united to produce from that earth comforts and luxuries, the expenditure on which rivals all the sums lavished on the other arts. Genius and practical skill has been brought into existence under the most marvellous circumstances, and when we consider that out of a natural substance, originally of unapparent value, productions have emanated, intrinsically worth more than if they had been formed of the precious metals, we may well conclude that a practical knowledge of, and a judicious taste for, the exquisite ceramic specimens dispersed throughout Europe, is not an unimportant result of civilization. Therefore let not the collector of so-termed bric-à-brac halt in his researches, the pursuit brings pleasure to himself, oft times profit, and is one of the least egotistical of tastes, as it also gives pleasure, instruction, and profit to others. Come with me, as many who love the treasures of art, and let us wander over Europe. I shall at times take you to odd places, and tell you strange stories, but you will be ever learning and never regretting. Come!

Böttcher, Harring, Morin, Lucca del Robbia, and Palissy, are my constant companions. Ay, and how full of interest is their society! how faithfully they recall the memory of past ages! and how fully they convince us that, despite all the go-ahead and vulgar presumption of the day in which we live, they may have rivals, yet have no equals either in taste or manipulation!

QUEST II.

HINTS TO BRIC-A-BRAC HUNTERS.

"There is no more potent antidote to low sensuality than the adoration of the beautiful.

"All the higher arts of design are essentially chaste without respect to the object.

"They purify the thoughts as tragedy purifies the passions. Their accidental effects are not worth consideration ; there are souls to whom even a vestal body is not holy."—SCHLEGEL.

SHOULD my readers agree with me in the sentiments thus written, many of them will be the more inclined to follow in my footsteps, or join me in many a ramble, replete with incident, in search of that which may be justly termed art treasures in other lands ; if so be not precisely in the hope of obtaining objects of higher art, to which I confess my heart has longed and hungered in vain, yet at least in search of the beautiful and attainable.

In days lang syne, when those who had the means and inclination were wont to visit foreign lands, the knowledge necessary to the search for bric-à-brac was confined to a limited circle. Moreover, the taste was by no means evinced as it is in the present day. Thus, pictures were purchased at high prices, and brought home as Murillos or Raphaels, Rubens or Titians, solely because they were purchased in Italy or Spain by those who had probably much more money than taste or discrimination; at all events little knowledge of pure art, or that refined and correct eye, granted by God and nurtured by practice, which could alone guide them. It is almost inconceivable what an amount of rubbish thus found its way to the rural homes of England and to the picture marts of the metropolis. It is true that a few possessing the requisite knowledge obtained prizes, while others made fortunes; but in those days they had a fine field, and little opposition. To-day such good fortune is rare indeed, and happy is the man who chances to meet with a gem. Porcelain was also purchased from every capital of Europe and the East, neither purchaser nor seller having much appreciation or knowledge of what they bought or sold; and thus, while now and then a charming specimen was obtained for a sum insignificant in reference to its real value, some worthless object was often purchased at a price given in these days for a perfect example of Sèvres or Capo di Monte.

Then, travellers went their way rejoicing in well-springed comfortable English carriages, driven by postilions in heavy quaint boots and long pigtails, content with what was, admiring all they saw, paying all that was asked of them, eating everything, and pronouncing it good because it was foreign, and gratefully acknowledging the well-paid-for civilities and courtesies they received—if they did receive them.

Many a high titled nobleman of our fatherland, many a possessor of broad acres, with a courier and interpreter in the rumble of his easy-going carriage, rushed from city to city, from river to lake, from snow-clad mountain to luxurious vale,—here, there, everywhere,—scarcely enjoying the beauties of nature granted by God, ignorant of one word of the language of the country through which he travelled. Having decided on the termination of his journey at a given spot, to that point he hastened, little caring how he got there, or at what cost; deterred neither by dirt nor by what might be justly called discomfort; enduring with a heroic resignation bad roads, bad hotels, and high charges. But *nous avons changé tout cela;* the fairest spots in Switzerland, the highest peak of the Alps, the most rugged pathways of the Apennines, the remotest German spas, the wildest fisheries of Norway, are now pervaded by the travelling Englishman. You meet your tailor at a picnic in the Black Forest; your bootmaker salutes you on the " castled crag of Drachenfels; " and if you elect to dine at a *table d'hôte*, you are apt to find yourself amidst a host of compatriots whom per-chance you may have met with in Cheapside or Whitechapel, when some untoward event may have called you to either of those localities. Bah! I would sooner go up in a balloon, or pass a week at Kovno on the banks of that historical river the Niemen.

Do not misunderstand me, my reader; hundreds of doubtless admirable people do now go abroad, whose grandfathers, nay fathers, scarcely knew that Malta was an island; and most unquestionably would have been plucked by the Civil Commissioners if requested to explain the position of Bodenbach, within so short a railway flight of that spot, where Böttcher, an apothecary's assistant, lived, and brought to light in 1755 the exquisite beauties of Dresden china.

And yet, forsooth, many of these doubtless amiable Saxons must have bric-à-brac, in order to show themselves equal in taste and refinement to my Lord This, the Duke of That, a Baron Rothschild, and other distinguished connoisseurs who are known to have collected glorious specimens of Wedgwood, Sèvres, or Majolica. And why not, if they really prize them, and have the means of obtaining them ? I do not refer to the money, inasmuch as half the tradesmen in the west-end of London or in Paris can wear three new hats to one of half the younger branches of England's nobility, and pay for them too. It is not a question of money. Real treasures are all but unobtainable ; or if met with, the price asked for them is so exorbitant, that the novice holds up his hands with astonishment or disgust ; and, being utterly unable to form a correct judgment of that combination of beauty and art which constitutes a perfect object, refuses the actual worth of his money, and only secures modern trash. I do not presume to say that there is not much that is beautiful and highly artistical in modern art ; but it has never been my good fortune to meet with anything to equal the purest specimens of ancient porcelain. The reason of our modern inferiority is clear. The celebrated artists who in other days painted on china were equal to the leading artists of the present era; and who among our leading great men, at home or abroad, would condescend to paint on china, save at a price that would make a cup or a vase equal in value to a first-rate picture?

Now we will suppose that a party of travellers arrive, we will say, at Dresden. They walk forth to visit the city, to see its justly acknowledged beauties, and, what is still more delightful to the feminine mind, its *shops*. Amongst these one of the first that attracts their attention is the emporium of a dealer in bric-à-brac. Miss Harriet gazes with delight at the cups and vases, with here and there a group, displayed in the window, and thus exclaims: "O, mamma dear, look at these lovely cups; are they not beautiful? While we are in Dresden, we must buy some Dresden china;" and so they enter, accompanied by a commissioner. There are commissioners and directors of all denominations in these days as thick as blackberries in autumn: fishery commis-

sioners, railway commissioners, travelling commissioners, and, alas, financial commissioners. But Miss
Harriet's commissioner is one of the class less aristo-
cratically called guides, or interpreters. The hotel
commissioner is a shabby-genteel gentleman, who,
like the rest of the world, will do anything for anyone—at his own price. Miss Harriet carefully
handles a cup, and exclaims on its unrivalled beauty ;
she gazes with rapture on a figure or a group; she
flutters admiringly over a *compotier;* while the
owner of these modern and moderate works of art
points out the marks : this of the Marcolini period,
and that used under the direction of Höroldt in 1720
—and so forth ; to the genuine nature of which signatures or warranties Mr. Commissioner very readily
testifies. So dear Harry, having expressed her
delight, becomes the possessor of some objects of art,
which she fondly supposes to be the rarest gems,
and which possibly form the commencement of a
collection destined to rival that of the late Mr.
Bernal or very many others—at least such is the
belief of dear Harry, as it is of a hundred other dear
Harrys and Georgies. "And pray, what *are* we to
believe in, if not in marks and signatures, mono-

grams and crossed daggers?" ask my fair bric-à-brac huntresses in despair. Alas, my dear young ladies, I regret to say that, amidst all the chicanery of this limited-liability and swindling era, there is none equal to that of a foreign bric-à-brac seller.

However, the cups and figures and so forth are purchased, carefully packed, and treasured as "the exquisite old china we bought in Dresden, my love— an enormous bargain, though the price seems very large to people who don't understand that kind of thing." And poor Miss Harriet remains happily un-conscious that similar treasures, ay and possibly far better, might have been purchased in the Strand for half the money; since I have no doubt dear Harry's "old" china was only recently produced at Meissen, that glorious manufactory, which all lovers of art ought to visit.

Now my object in writing these pages is to offer some practical remarks, which may tend to aid the inexperienced lover of bric-à-brac in his researches. Not for one moment, however, do I presume to call myself a first-rate judge. Many and many a blunder have I made; and sorely have I paid for my apprenticeship. Often have I become the possessor of some piece of trumpery, which in my vanity I believed to be a priceless treasure. Indeed, I am satisfied that there are few connoisseurs living, whatever their knowledge or experience, who are not at times deceived—I do not say as to their judgment of beauty and outline or execution, but as to period and country. Beautiful as are many of our specimens in the Kensington Museum, there is only one person connected with that institution—and I say so with no intentional discourtesy—in whom I should have great faith as a purchaser. Much that is good has been refused at moderate prices, and much that is mediocre obtained at heavy ones. Indeed the taste and knowledge of many of the leading dealers of London render them better judges than the best of amateurs. And this is only natural; for is it not their daily, nay hourly, business?—a business in which they hazard thousands, and from which they sometimes realise fortunes. Before starting on our first bric-à-brac quest, I would unhesitatingly say, that for all moderate specimens of ceramic art there is no place so cheap, be it where it may, as London; while in that city the highest price is obtainable for the finest specimens. In Paris, good, bad, and indifferent objects are all alike dear, unless that fickle goddess Fortune, who does at times befriend you, gives you a helping hand. But we will leave these great emporiums of bric-à-brac for the present, and take our first trip eastward—not quite so far east as China or Japan, but to the Sublime Porte, where we will pass a pleasant morning in the Persian Bazaar, which, by the way, is by some termed the Arms Bazaar.

When, in my earliest boyhood, as I have already said, I was wont to fancy that all porcelain, of whatever kind, was the produce of China and Japan, I had, at least, some slight justification for my idea, since in those kingdoms it no doubt originated. Porcelain is an intermediate substance between pottery and glass,—more translucent than the one, more opaque than the other,—and is presumed to be of Chinese origin, its manufacture dating from so early a period as the beginning of the Christian era. Be this as it may, there is evidence of its use in the fifteenth century and in the beginning of the fourteenth. The famous tower of porcelain at Nankin was built three hundred and thirty feet

high, and still stands. It consists of nine stories of
enamelled bricks or tiles, in five colours,—white,
red, blue, green, and brown. Japanese china existed
at almost as remote a period, and was perhaps in all
respects finer than Chinese; while in the days of
Queen Anne and the first Georges china vases,
dishes, and hideous monsters, were to be seen in all
the houses of the rich in old England.

As I grew older, however, I learnt another lesson ;
and although I fully admit the rare beauty of many
of the productions of China and Japan, both modern
and ancient, and am aware that fine specimens still
command high prices, I confess that European
specimens are far more agreeable to my taste ; and I
fancy the Oriental china now in the market, which
if gathered together would more than fill the Crystal
Palace or two Crystal Palaces, is no longer valued as
it was wont to be. There was, indeed, a period
when the china termed " crackles " was highly ap-
preciated, and when specimens of that ware sold for
more than their weight in silver. But now even the
finest specimens appear to be of no great value ; so
capricious is taste, or fashion, or whatever you like
to call that inconstant deity whose wand rules the

desires of Belgravian mankind. It is not long since I acquired a practical knowledge of this fact. Happening to have in my possession two small crackle vases, one green, the other yellow, and wishing to get rid of them, I took them to a dealer, expecting a large price for them. Judge my surprise when he offered me two pounds for my treasures, with the assurance that his profit would not be ten shillings; and I have had from subsequent experience no just reason to doubt him.

Indeed, a gallant friend of mine, who had been present at that which may be fairly termed the ransacking of the Palace of Pekin, informed me only recently that he had brought home some fine specimens of Japan and Oriental china, most of which he had sold in London for at least a third less than he could have obtained from the natives ere he left; and he added, "If all the specimens, good, bad, and indifferent, which now overburden the English market were returned from whence they came, they would sell for double the price to be obtained either in London or in any other of the European capitals. In fact, the natives are highly indignant that so much which is precious to them

should leave the country." Some of our largest
collectors or dealers may act on this hint, if so
minded. I place the suggestion unreservedly at
their service.

Although it is my intention to dwell more largely
on the subject of china—which is my peculiar taste
—in subsequent pages, than others, articles of the
fine arts, carved ivory, Venetian and Bohemian
glass, wood carvings, arms, and ancient jewelry, may
all come fairly under the denomination of bric-à-
brac.

QUEST III.

ONE ounce of practice is worth ten of theory,—at least so said some practical philosopher of old time; and I fully agree with him.

We are at Marseilles. The getting there in the merry month of May, when vineyards and mulberry-trees put forth their early leaves, and almond-trees are in full bloom, is a pleasant and unfatiguing journey. Few, if any, are the railways in Europe by which one travels so smoothly or arrives with such punctuality as on the line between Paris and Marseilles. We leave the former city at 8 P.M., and arrive at the latter on the following day at noon; so that little delay is allowed for gastronomy *en route.* A cup of *café-au-lait* at that city of democracy, Lyons—where the waiters go round the table for payment ere you have swallowed the first spoonful of your beverage—is all that you can expect till the journey ends; unless, indeed, you snatch up a slice

of truffled pie during your three minutes' halt at
Avignon—a halt just long enough to make you
regret that you cannot linger for a late breakfast at
that unrivalled buffet, where the civility of the
proprietor is only surpassed by the excellency of his
supplies.

The Marseilles of to-day is no more the Marseilles
of our grandfathers, nor indeed of our fathers, than
is the Paris of Napoleon III. the Paris of Napoleon I.
Nevertheless there are few cities in Europe which,
at all times and under all circumstances, present
more stirring life.   In this southern port men of all
tongues and all nations throng together in commercial enterprise.   The traveller is almost bewildered
by the clamour of strange sounds ; while dark and
swarthy Saracenic countenances remind him that he
is approaching Oriental Europe.

The heights that rise above the city are clad with
the dark verdure of olives and pines, that seem to
spring from a barren waste.   Amid these sombre
groves are scattered innumerable white-washed and
green-shuttered "bastides," or villas, occupied by
the Marseilles citizens.   The town itself appears to
repose at your feet, if indeed the word repose may

be applied to that boiling, seething port; the outline of the coast being broken by a regular basin
communicating by a narrow neck with the sea.

This basin produced the city. The Greeks of old
found out its advantages, and their temples and
shrines marked the inlet from the Mediterranean
Sea. Old Marsalia flourished like new Marseilles.
The harbour was and is its heart, the salt-water its
life-blood. A strange and peculiar contrast is produced by the dusty gray of the houses and the deep
blue of this inland basin of sea.

The ocean is in the very centre of the town; the
buildings fence it in and encircle the harbour. It
lies as if sleeping in this embrace—perhaps the one
instance of a great city built in a circle broken only
by one small opening. Beyond, you behold rocky
hills—hard, hot, glaring; parched in midsummer, in
mid-winter bare, barren, and bleak. All round and
about Marseilles they rise, all along the sea-coast
you observe them glancing and flashing in the
bright scorching air; not, however, entirely without
verdure, sombre, unpleasing, and unrefreshing though
it be to the eye.

Yet if the land be dark, burnt, and barren, what a

splendid contrast presents itself in the glorious
ocean, whose liquid azure is so profound as to
become almost imperial purple !

Descend once more into the city; observe the old
harbour and the new. They were alike harbours
and cesspools; all the drainings of the vastly-popu-
lated city originally poured into them, and filled the
air with pestilence and disease. Such had been the
case for ages; and as no tide stirs the Mediterranean,
there the foul sewage lay and rotted and stagnated,
and from thence its miasmatic vapours rose to
spread fever and death.

No wonder, then, that cholera should so often
have smitten the city with a strong and blighting
hand. Yet beyond these stagnant pestilential lakes
the breeze comes dancing freely over the ocean—at
times far too freely for those about to embark on its
troubled waters—and the waves are as pure as salt-
water waves can be.

Graceful feluccas skim over the waters, bending
under their striped canvas, while steamers of all
nations and ships-of-war are dotted over the sea.
All is life, motion, and varied colouring. The forest
of masts, the deep-blue sea, and the bright-blue sky,

seen under favourable circumstances, form altogether a picture not easily forgotten.

Such was the Marsalia of yesterday; such, in many respects, is the Marseilles of to-day. And yet, as in the case of Vienna or Paris, he that has not journeyed there for ten years past will find a new, ay and a splendid city risen on the foundations of the old. The Canébière is a noble street; a grand cathedral rises day by day in vast proportions. The New Exchange or Bourse is a handsome pile; and, best improvement of all, the sanitary state of the city is much amended and now well cared for. The whole of the infectious substance, heretofore allowed to collect in the streets till it rotted and was thence carried off by violent rains into the harbours, is now daily collected and removed to the country for agricultural purposes. A new harbour of considerable dimensions is completed; and the sewage, flowing through greatly - improved drains, is no longer allowed to pour itself into the harbours. For which blessed improvement the inhabitants may cheerfully pay and be thankful.

So much for this proud city, which bids fair to rival the chief commercial cities of Europe.

Is there a traveller who wanders to foreign lands
for health, business, pleasure, or bric-à-brac hunting,
who does not expect ease at his inn, and who,
having swallowed and paid for a pound of grease or
a quart of oil, and endured a brief martyrdom from
dirt, vermin, and bad attendance, does not quarrel
with his lot and the authors of it, and mark with a
double cross in his journal the entry which warns
him to avoid the Blue Boar or L'Aigle d'Or, as the
case may be, for the future ?

I am no sybarite, yet I confess to a love for
comfort and cleanliness in my caravanserai. I am
no *gourmet*, but I own that for perfect comfort I
prefer an hotel where the chief cook is an artist. I
may therefore as well remark that at Marseilles I
should select for choice the Hôtel de Marseilles or
the Petit Louvre. I know it is the fashion—alas,
who leads the way that so many are wont to follow ?
—to select the Grand Hôtel de Paris or the Grand
Hôtel de Louvre ; but experience tells me that the
grandeur generally exists only in the outward
appearance of the house.

So, having ordered a moderate repast to satisfy
the inner man at the Petit Louvre—giving strict

orders for the exclusion of all provincial *plats*, for the inhabitants of the city are much given to oil, raw artichokes, and olives—let us walk forth to see the sights and visit the bric-à-brac shops.

As yet, though my visits to the commercial city have been frequent, I have only discovered four such shops at Marseilles. They are as follows: Esmeir, Rue Parcellis 22 ; Valli, Rue de Paradis 24; Pardieu, No. 43 in the same street; and Sondier, Rue Masquire. There is little to choose between these dealers, though the two first are generally the best supplied. Their knowledge, however, of the art gems they profess to sell is very mediocre, and their prices most exorbitant; nevertheless, the very fact of their comparative ignorance is the best chance for the practical buyer, who thus, if the wind be in his favour, may chance to carry off something worthy his collection. And as for the price demanded—bah! was there ever a correctly-judging bric-à-bric hunter who had not the courage to offer about one-half, say one-third, of the price demanded ? or was there ever a seller who had the honesty to refuse the bid ? Of course I by no means include in these sweeping

opinions the higher class of dealers, the sellers of
first-class *objets d'art.*

With reference to those of Marseilles, I neither
wish to be uncourteous nor unkind when I say they
are by no means to be found in that society. The
wherefore is easily explained. The Marseillais taste,
among rich or poor, high or low, male or female, does
not rank high ; in fact, the city is essentially demo-
cratic in taste as in politics. Ponderous furniture,
modern pictures and modern china, big vases, much
gilding, gorgeous colouring, an excessive gaudiness
both in dress and decoration, with little art or
beauty, prevail in that commercial hemisphere. The
wealthy trader of Marseilles would pass by a lovely
specimen of Wedgwood or Capo di Monte, and
purchase some modern abomination in French china
highly decorated and gilded, to adorn his rooms ;
while his wife, if he have one, would select the most
gorgeous silk and the brightest Persian shawl with
which to bedeck her person. Thus it is not often
that anything really worthy of being added to an
amateur collection is to be secured in this city. It
by no means follows, however, that gems are not
occasionally met with here ; and he who loves such

acquisitions never neglects the smallest chance of a bargain. Nor should the collector on any account fail to explore the emporiums of Marseilles. I shall endeavour to explain the why and the wherefore.

Marseilles is essentially a thoroughfare to and from the East, as well as to Spain and Italy, by the water-route, and hundreds are wise enough to know that art treasures can be disposed of *en passant* there as elsewhere. Consequently various ceramic specimens do find their way into the hands of the dealers, from whom they pass onwards to Paris at a premium, not seldom being cheaply purchased and dearly sold. Now, if you can only stop a Capo di Monte group on its way from Italy, or a Bueno Retiro vase from Spain, or aught else, before it takes flight to the imperial city, which on more than one occasion it has been my good fortune to do, it will well repay you the trouble of an hour's visit to the bric-à-brac shops of the Rue de Paradis.

La Provence could formerly boast of several manufactures of pottery ; but not till the end of the seventeenth century did it produce glazed or enamelled pottery, some time after that of Moustiers.

The first fabricant at Marseilles was Jean Delarisse in 1769; whereas in the middle of the eighteenth century there were several artists, some of whom produced enamelled pottery.

Robert of Marseilles was another distinguished name. His works were first produced in 1793.

The widow Perrin, or Madame Perrin Veuve, as she was called, was, I believe, the last celebrated producer. Many specimens of her ware may still be found, which are very interesting. They are generally marked with a monogram of the letters V. P. (Veuve Perrin.)

And now, the weather being fine and the sea calm, say in the latter end of May and early June, the trip by sail or steamer to Messina is not the most unpleasant undertaking in life; moreover, it is of short duration. I am not aware as to whether the patriotism of Garibaldi ever moved him to collect the art treasures of the country he loves so well; but you get a view of his solitary mansion as you pass through the Straits of Bonifacio, perched as it is on a lonely and verdurous spot on the rocky island of Caprera, and possibly say to yourself,

having recently strolled up Regent-street or the
Boulevards, "Though I should die of ennui or go
mad were my residence fixed here through the
winter, during summer a yacht and books might
make it endurable."

There is no doubt that the position of Messina is
a lovely one, placed as it is in a mild and pleasant
climate; but it would be far more so if the city were
backed with some glorious oaks, and the country
around and about were overshadowed with such
woodlands as old England alone can boast of. I
dwell for a moment on the beauties of nature, inasmuch as no real lover of art can be unmindful of
those beauties, from which all that is precious in
taste or design emanates. In fact, the study of
art gives the mind a keener insight into nature's
charms, and teaches us to observe and appreciate
them justly.

All therefore I desire to remark *en passant*, when
travelling to the East, in reference to Messina, is
that it ever appears to me as the last spot *en route*
on which a feeling of civilization rests, and on
returning, the first. It contains, however, a fountain
of great beauty in the public square, which bad

taste has somewhat destroyed by restoration. I had a photograph taken of it, with the intention of submitting it to Minton or at Miessen, as, modelled and produced in china, it would make an exquisite centre piece.

Of bric-à-brac shops I have as yet never discovered one at Messina; still there is a gentleman who has had the good taste to be a collector of such gems as chance has brought to him from other lands. These he is courteously willing to show, and by no means unwilling to sell, to the stranger. I therefore feel fortunate in having made his acquaintance; and I suggest to all bric-à-brac hunters who may pass through Scylla and Charybdis to follow my example.

I owe him a debt of gratitude; but as he himself is entirely ignorant of the fact, I am by no means called on to repay it, and shall only be too glad, should circumstances lead me once more to his abode, if he will do me a similar kindness, inasmuch as he sold me an exquisite Bueno Retiro cup—saucerless, it is true—which was worth as many pounds sterling as I paid francs.

Finding myself on board one of the Messagerie steamers *en route* to Marseilles, I made the acquain-

tance of an agreeable little French doctor of medicine, whose taste, if not experience, was similar to
my own; and having suggested a raid on shore at
Messina in search of anything in the ceramic line
which might turn up, I fortunately introduced him
to the "baron," for such was the title our friend
claimed. Whether he was a baron of the Roman
empire or a Sicilian noble was of slight importance.
He had pictures, such as they were,—Majolica,
Grecian pottery, and some trifles in porcelain; all of
which were at our service—for a consideration.

Having offered the usual courtesies which polite
society dictates, I requested to be informed if he had
any specimens of china to dispose of.

"Nothing but a few cups, signor," he replied;
"here they are."

I forthwith selected four, three of little value.
The fourth I at once knew to be a prize, it being a
charming Bueno Retiro cup, on which was an
exquisitely painted battle-scene. Having demanded
the price of the four—which being five francs each,
I immediately paid without comment,—and then
having looked round the rooms and thanked our
host, we wished him good morning, as our vessel

was about to sail. Ere leaving, however, I placed three of the cups carelessly in my coat-pockets, retaining the other carefully in my hand. No sooner was the street-door closed on us than the little doctor exclaimed,

"*Parbleu, mon ami,* that appears to be a nice cup; moreover, you take particular care of it. *Voulez-vous me le céder?* I will give you ten francs for it."

"Not for a hundred," said I.

When on board I bade him carefully examine the painting with a magnifying glass; and then he broke forth into French expressions very difficult to translate, but which in English might mean, "By jingo, it is a beauty! How tenderly you handled it!" adding, "Why, I had it in my hand first; but as you made no remark, I fancied it was no better than those you put like oranges in your pockets."

"Precisely, doctor," I replied; "practice and experience give knowledge. When next you visit the baron, look sharper."

I had a little box made when on board, wrapped up my cup in cotton, consoled the doctor by presenting him one of the others, and took it to England;

where, as at Paris, it was valued at from five to six pounds. Thus, my friends, be advised, and never allow a chance to escape you when bric-à-brac hunting.

QUEST IV.

STAMBOUL.

AND now let us steam onwards to the city of the Sultan.

Before the outbreak of the Crimean war, there was no lack of fine specimens of Oriental china in the bazaars at Constántinople; and here and there a good specimen of Sèvres, Dresden, Italian ware, and even specimens of Wedgwood and Worcester, might be secured. Meanwhile, among the multitude, military, naval, and civil, who then found themselves in that which at the period was an Eastern capital, but to-day has put on, forsooth, as far as the Frank portion is concerned, the very worst features of modern civilization, fast obliterating all the interest formerly derived from its Oriental character, there were naturally not only men with taste, and lovers of art, but also men with money without taste or knowledge. Therefore were the bazaars ransacked, and good, bad, and indifferent specimens vanished day by bay. Moreover, Turks, Armenians, Persians, and Jews had but one object in view—that of robbing the Giaours, as the officers of her Majesty's army were called, to the utmost possible extent. And while on the one hand most if not all the buyers were more or less ignorant of the fact that, when asked a hundred piastres—which in some cases might not have been an exorbitant price for the object desired, and was therefore readily given— had they been wise enough to offer twenty-five, the sum would have been cheerfully accepted.

Again, the sellers were more or less equally ignorant of the value of that which they sold. It was therefore by no means difficult, having know- ledge and experience, every now and then to obtain a gem at a very reasonable—at times, indeed, ridiculously small—outlay. But a change soon came over the dream of both buyers and sellers. The buyers, at the suggestion of interpreters or commissioners,—who all acted in the spirit of robbery, and stood the friend of either the one or the other, who paid most freely,—would, as I have said, offer twenty piastres where a hundred had been asked ; and so the sellers soon settled the matter by

demanding double, conceiving, as they all did, that
an Englishman was not made of flesh and blood, but
of gold, and that pieces might be chipped off him as
off stone. More: it soon got abroad that the
Giaour would buy a tin pot for a sovereign if he
were only told it was an ancient specimen from
Damascus, or a china cup which he might have
purchased in England for a shilling, if informed it
was Dresden, or "Sax," as they term it. And the
market soon became glutted with the most inconceivable rubbish, much of which found its way back
to England and France, whence it originally came,
having meanwhile been purchased at a hundred per
cent. more than its real value.

Long years have elapsed since those painful, yet
at times merry days of war and love. And now,
while the Sublime Porte has endeavoured to brighten
its face with the varnish of civilization, thus making
it far more dirty than it was wont to be, the bazaars,
with equal unsuccess, have in a great measure
followed the European example. Let us pass a
morning therein. If, however, you have not physical
powers, patience, and temper, you had better remain
at home, whether the season of your visit be winter

or summer; for of all the fatiguing pleasures in life
I know of, there are none equal to a day's bric-à-
brac hunting in the bazaars of Constantinople.
Moreover, in the present year, unless you are greatly
favoured by fortune—or by luck, if you prefer to call
it so—after all your patience, trials of temper, and
fatigues, you may return home without a single
addition to your collection.

Now the bazaar in the city of the Sultan, as in all
other Eastern towns, as all the travelled world is
aware, is simply that portion of the town set apart
more particularly for the retail trade of every
possible article of Eastern and European produce;
and it is also more or less the habitation of those
useful relations, termed in common parlance Uncles,
or Israelites; kind friends who claim, by imaginary
blood, the right of lending you five shillings on a
watch which cost you five pounds,—of course giving
you a tolerably bad chance of redeeming it. It is
also, to some extent, a depôt for the reception of
stolen goods. No; I will not be severe. I merely
mean to say that if a pasha who has an over-
abundance of Dresden, or Eastern, or even Sèvres
china, desires his attendant to dust it, two or three

pieces may possibly be broken in the dusting, or said
to be so, and sent to the bazaar to be mended,
whence they never return to their rightful owner.
I have not unfrequently been informed that there
is a vast amount of ceramic treasure in the harems,
as in the houses, of the rich pashas, much of which
from time to time finds its way to the bazaar. Now,
it is perfectly true that the amount of Sèvres coffee-
cups, Dresden china, Oriental vases, and so forth,
gathered together in the houses of the rich Turks, is
probably immense, though for the most part modern,
and of no particular value. And so, without fear of
contradiction, I assert, that if the whole were placed
before the eager gaze of a real connoisseur, he would
not among the lot select a score of objects worthy of
consideration. I will tell you why it is so, my
friends, whom I more particularly desire should be
successful in those researches which I so much love.
It is simply because, with very rare exceptions, the
Eastern taste, like that of Marseilles, is vulgar and
gorgeous in gold and colouring ; and I very much
doubt if the Sultan—I beg his pardon, the light of
the world—the grand vizier, the pasha with fifty
tails, or the choicest beauties of their harems—are

competent to judge, or care whether the gorgeous china that adorns their rooms, or the pretty jewelled cups from which they sip their coffee, or the dishes in which they dip their delicate hands, are made at Dresden, Pekin, Sèvres, or England; whether they be of hard paste or soft; what marks they bear; in what year they were produced; or who the artist that decorated them. Indeed, a vast quantity of porcelain is made, and has been made, at Meissen, Vienna, and elsewhere, purposely for the Eastern markets, which is marked, truly, but of particular forms, for particular purposes, to contain meats, vegetables, and sweetmeats; and this is immediately known to an experienced hunter, and rarely found elsewhere. It is true that here and there a fine specimen may be secured, and of such it has been my good fortune to collect a few. Generally speaking, however, the painting is coarse, the forms neither artistic nor tasteful, and of little value to those who look for beauty of decoration, chasteness in outline, and delicacy of execution.

In bidding adieu to the Eastern capital, I by no means recommend a visit to the bazaar, if merely in pursuit of ceramic treasures. I have, it is true, from

time to time picked up a piece of Worcester, Wedgwood, and Dresden, at moderate prices; no doubt
brought to Constantinople in other days by an
ambassador, consul-general, or some English merchant; but little now remains, and for such as there
is to be found, the price asked is double that for
which the same objects may be purchased in London.
The fashion for collecting bric-à-brac without practice
or knowledge has caused this. No sooner does an
Englishman present himself in the bazaars than he
is pounced upon by a host of greedy, unsavoury-
smelling interpreters, who vie with one another in
the endeavour to pillage him, and who generally
succeed. Now, the readers of these pages must
permit me to introduce them to Mr. Zenope, in the
Grand Bazaar, a most respectable Armenian. If you
visit Stamboul, porcelain-loving reader, go direct to
him, place yourself unreservedly in his hands,
decline all Jewish assistance, and I, after many
years' experience, will answer for his honesty and
probity.

Meanwhile permit me to remark that scarcely any
physical undertaking is more fatiguing than that of
passing a day of research in the bazaars of Stamboul,

particularly if you are not so fortunate as to find aught that is satisfactory.

The mode and manner of Oriental dealing is wide apart from that which may be simply termed European buying and selling. In London, Paris, or Vienna, you enter a bric-à-brac shop; its contents are, generally speaking, clear to the eye; you select that which appears to be desirable, ask the price, make your offer, purchase or refuse, and go your way. I must confess I should scarcely have the courage to act in London as I should unquestionably be disposed to do either at Paris or Vienna, or indeed any other Continental capital or town, namely, offer about half or a third the price asked. But all such delicate ideas may be banished in the bazaars at Constantinople, with the assurance that you will obtain nothing, great or small, on which some profit has not been secured to the sellers.

Having paid your respects to Zenope, accepted a cup of Turkish coffee or a glass of lemonade, according to season and inclination, smoked a cheroot or cigarette—if given to cigarettes, to which all the Frank inhabitants incline—proceed to that portion of the bazaars entitled the Arms Bazaar. It is dark,

gloomy, not to say dirty, to the eye, and unsavoury
to the nose, but curious and picturesque in the
extreme.   .

You approach the shop, if it may so be called, of
a bric-à-brac merchant. He is possibly engaged
with some other customer, or smoking his pipe, or
munching a cucumber, or counting his beads, and
takes no more notice of you than if you were one of
the dogs that lie sleeping in the streets of Stamboul.
Patience is said to be a virtue—prove that you
possess it if you can, and bring all your good-temper
to aid you. Being in a hurry will not assist you in
the slightest degree. If the dealer's tongue be
unknown to you, appeal calmly for the aid of your
interpreter, and arouse the old gentleman from his
lethargy as you would stir up a sleepy animal in
Wombwell's menagerie.   .

You see, or fancy you see, high on the shelf above
him, a choice piece of china, or any other article of
bric-à-brac, which might possibly suit you ; and as it
is in all probability covered with dust, and beyond
your reach, you civilly request to be permitted to
handle it prior to the investment of your money.
In answer to your request, the merchant casts his.

expressive eyes towards the roof of the bazaar, and
gives a kind of cluck with his throat, which means
that the object is either broken or already sold, or
that in his opinion it will not please you. The fact
of the matter is, the weather is hot, and moving is
unpleasant. Being, however, desirous to judge for
yourself, you again politely rouse his Excellency, who
at length uncrosses his legs, raises himself from his
sitting position, and does you the favour to allow
you to examine the goods he is there to sell, with
the air of a man who is doing you an honour. We
will say that you take a fancy to some object
amongst his wares. Then comes the bargaining·
Alas, this is a diplomatic process almost beyond
European endurance. "Ask him the price," you say
to your interpreter. The free-and-easy merchant
chumps his cucumber or smokes his pipe, as he
calmly replies, "Two hundred piastres." "Two
hundred piastres! Why, I could buy it in Vienna
for fifty!" you exclaim. "No doubt, sir," says the.
disinterested interpreter; "but you are in Stamboul,
not in Vienna." And so you move on, and, nine
times out of ten, are called back, and possibly end
by making the purchase for about a quarter the

price first named. And so is it throughout the
bazaars.

Turks are neither an energetic nor an inventive
people; neither are they gifted with taste for, or
love of, the fine arts. I should scarcely imagine that
a hundred subjects of the Light of the World could
distinguish a Murillo from a signboard, or a Sèvres
vase from a flower-pot. Nevertheless there was a
porcelain manufactory formerly on the banks of the
Bosphorus, the property, I fancy, of foreigners. I do
not suppose, however, that it succeeded in achieving
much beyond a teapot or washhand-basin, though I
possess a small jug said to be of Turkish manufacture, not ungraceful. And yet I know of no
country on which the sun shines that possesses such
abundance of admirable material for the manufac-
turing of pottery and porcelain. Had poor Palissy
lived in the East, what marvels of art he would have
produced! But the art of Turkey scarcely soars
above a gilded pipe-bowl.

QUEST V.

MADRID.

"Quen dice Espagna dice toto."

" No hay sino un Madrid " (There is but one Madrid). There is but one stage from Madrid to Paradise, in which there is a window for angels to look down on the counterpart of heaven on earth. So say all Spaniards. Have you ever been there? No. Well, the month is late spring, the sky blue, the sea calm and purple; so let us start—say from Marseilles; cross the oft-times troubled waters of the Gulf of Lyons, now like a mirror; touch at Barcelona, where I never yet saw or cracked a nut; halt at Alicant; and travel south by railway through La Manca, mentally in company with Don Quixote and Sancho, to the capital of her most Catholic Majesty. Though it is at times the hottest, and at others the coldest climate in southern Europe— indeed, it is proverbially asserted that *"el aire de Madrid es tan sotil, que mata a un hombre, y no*

apaya a un candil," which being translated simply
means that the subtle air which will not extinguish
a candle puts out a man's life—it is nevertheless by
no means an indifferent abiding-place for a time for
the bric-à-brac hunter, or anyone else.

The position of Madrid is unique ; it may be fairly
said, in the middle of a desert. All the great capitals
of Europe denote as it were of their position,
and are announced to the traveller by their populated environs, which bespeak the vitality of the
city.

Madrid, on the contrary, is like a planet lost in
space, which shines without lighting you ; without
wood ; till recently, without water ; without stone ;
without an industrious population ; without commerce, save that which supplies its luxuries.

Madrid, when first approached, gives you the idea
of effect without cause—a sort of royal caprice
unaided by nature ; in other days it was simply a
fortified burgh, which, nevertheless, could boast
the honour of being besieged by the Cid. King
Philip the Second proclaimed it the seat of
government, and a rendezvous for sport.

He desired to make it a city ; it has never been

anything but a Court, from which it has derived the only influence which brings great cities to life.

After having passed, we will say, a week in the Museo, with which time, if you are a lover of high art, you will still scarcely be satisfied, so exceedingly rich is the place in treasures—a palace in fact of thought and beauty, filled with spirits of past days, where the dead reappear as in visions of delight;—as a refreshment for your taxed energies, seek the walks of the Retiro gardens, near which was the celebrated "La China," or royal porcelain manufactory, founded by Charles III. in 1759, who brought workmen from his similar factory at Capo di Monte, Naples. Everything was destroyed by the French, and the place converted into a fortification, which surrendered with 200 cannon, on the 14th August, 1812, to the Iron Duke. It was subsequently blown up by Lord Hill, when the misconduct, or perfidy, or whatever you like to call it, of Ballesteros compelled him to evacuate Madrid. Since which time, to the day in which we live and hunt for specimens of Bueno Retiro, one of the standing calumnies against us—so often repeated, and still credited by young Spain, although more than half a century has elapsed—is that all the finest specimens were destroyed by the English from mere jealousy. Whereas the real truth is that the fathers, or grandfathers, of our gallant allies of to-day scarcely recollect what they did yesterday—they broke the Ollas themselves, and converted the manufactory into a Bastille, which, and not the pipkins, we did destroy. So little did we dread Spanish competition, which might well be dreaded if Spain could produce, in 1868, such specimens as those once issued from "La China," that we have actually introduced their system; and very fair china is now produced at Madrid, made for the most part by English workmen.

Ferdinand VII., on his restoration, re-created "La China," removing the workshops and warerooms to La Mondoa; but this has also ceased to exist—at least as regards high art.

On my first visit to Madrid—or La Corte, as it is generally termed by Spaniards, as if there were no other court in Europe save that of the Spanish Paradise or La Gloria—I own my heart beat with fond anticipation of the numberless specimens of Bueno Retiro china I should carry homewards. But, alas, such was my ignorance of this extremely rare and beautiful porcelain, that all my researches were more or less in vain. I obtained little or nothing worthy to be purchased ; and with the exception of a few very moderate and imperfect specimens, I have never been enabled to secure anything of great beauty. In fact, the only group of real value that I cast my eyes on at Madrid was a centre-piece on the English minister's table, which, when hungry, one hardly thanked him for exhibiting; for while, on the one hand, it created envy and jealousy, on the other, the impossibility of keeping one's longing eyes from it prevented due attention to his gastronomic hospitality.

In other days there were three very indifferent bric-à-brac shops at Madrid. One was more or less a private collection, though everything was for sale that was gathered together by Don Hosez, landlord of the Hôtel d'Angleterre, the only decent hotel both as regards charges and comfort I ever recollect at Madrid. Don Hosez's establishment was opposite the British Legation, in the ancient palace or judgment-hall of the Inquisition. But both Don Hosez and his hotel have ceased to exist, and

happily the Inquisition also. The house has become
the residence of the French ambassador, and Don·
Hosez's collection has since been scattered far and
wide. From him I chanced to get a few pieces of
Spanish pottery and porcelain of little value. One
of the other shops appears also to have vanished ;
and on my last visit to La Corte, I only discovered
the third in the Calle Alcaza, where little is to be
obtained, save an occasional sword, and various
heavy and by no means choice specimens of mediæval
furniture.

Some years ago, when strolling leisurely one
intensely hot evening in August along the Calle
Alcaza, the very best if not the principal street of
Madrid, I chanced to see some curious cups in the
window of the shop in question. After examining
them, and asking their value, I suggested to the
owner that, as it was late and my dinner awaited me,
if he would send them to my hotel on the following
morning, I would make him an offer. To this he
agreed, and expressed a desire to show me a handsome china *déjeûner* then in his possession. " It is
late and getting dark," said I ; nevertheless I could
not resist a peep ; and so, after traversing several

dark passages, we entered a room filled with aucient dusty furniture, when a cupboard being unlocked, he produced therefrom a large brass-bound box, which contained, as he had said, a *déjeûner* of the most lovely modern Sèvres it has ever been my good fortune to behold. Having taken one of the pieces in my hand and examined the mark, I carelessly asked the price, which being named I found far beyond my means and intentions. Nevertheless the owner appeared extremely anxious to part with it; and as I bade him good-evening, he urged me to come again by day-light. "Well," I replied, "it is very beautiful, though quite modern; moreover, if it were not so, your price is at least two-thirds beyond what I should be disposed to give." "Maybe; but the signor will at all events call to-morrow?" "Possibly," said I. And so we parted, not, however, without a lingering desire on my part to possess the *déjeûner*, however small the hope. I felt besides an intense curiosity as to how he had obtained it; for it was far too costly to have come, as I supposed, honestly into the hands of him who claimed it.

On the following morning a Signorina, somewhat

fat and certainly over forty, accompanied by a lad, called on me with the few specimens I had selected, which, after a little bargaining, became my property ; and she then urged on me to take another look at the Sèvres, which I agreed to do, appointing three o'clock as the time of my visit. On my arrival, having passed along the same dark passages, which were divided by doors, the china was again placed before me, and there being a much brighter light, it appeared still more beautiful than on the previous evening. In the room at the time there were two women and the lad who had brought my china in the morning. Having again questioned her as to the price, &c., I told the good woman who appeared to take the lead, that I did not want the china (which was an innocent fib), that it was far beyond my means ; but, said I, in an off-hand manner, "as you appear most anxious to part with it, I will tell you what I will do—I will give you forty sovereigns, or fifty napoleons in gold ; " gold being then some-what scarce at Madrid. Now my offer was received with great good-humour, but neither accepted nor refused—in fact, made half in joke, half in earnest, more than 200*l.* having been demanded. I then began to look at some old swords which lay dusty in a corner of the apartment ; when all of a sudden the door flew open, and in rushed two of the most disagreeable-looking vagabonds I ever beheld. Drawing, as if by impulse, the sword I held in my hand from the scabbard, the Spanish proverb occurred to me, "*No me sagues sin razon ; no me envaines sino honor ; *" which simply means, Do not draw me without cause, or sheath me without honour; and dropping the point, I stood with my back to the corner from whence I had taken it awaiting the next move—not, however, very calmly, for the day was intensely hot, and it occurred to me that I had got into a den of thieves. Moreover, an angry Spaniard is not always particular whether he sticks you in the back or the front. But what did it all mean? The two men appeared to be terribly excited, and the angry discussion in *patois* which took place was far beyond my comprehension, though I and the box of china were evidently the subjects of discussion. My position, I must admit, was not the pleasantest in life. At last, a temporary pause taking place, I demanded the cause of this inconceivable outbreak. " We were behind the door," said one man, " and we

heard you offer fifty sovereigns for the china."
" You are in error," said I; " I offered fifty napoleons.
Nevertheless, if you will bring it to my hotel, I will
give you fifty sovereigns,"—glad to escape by any
means from my disagreeable position; "I do not
carry so much gold in my pocket."

On this another boisterous conversation took
place, the box and its contents being eventually
hoisted on one man's shoulders; and I hailed the
fact as the advent of my release and possession of
the china. But, alas, nothing of the kind. I was
detained another half-hour—a prisoner in fact.
Happily my release came at last in the person of a
well-dressed gentleman, who had doubtless been sent
for, and who evidently had a perfect knowledge of
my gaolers, and also of the china I was desirous to
purchase. Having at length gained the street, I
addressed my companion, courteously demanding
whom I had the honour to thank for my release,
what was his connection with the parties by whom I
had been insulted—in fact, I requested to be enlightened as to the whole affair.

Thus spoke the mighty hidalgo, having first informed me he was a Spanish nobleman :

"You ought not to trust yourself in such places."

"Trust myself in such places!" I replied; "a bric-à-brac shop in the principal street and thorough-fare of Madrid?" .

"You are not in England, signor," he replied.

"There is no question as to that," I said; "mean-while I thank you for coming to my aid, whether intentionally or by chance. I am ignorant of your knowledge of these people, and equally so of your connection in reference to the china they so eagerly desire to sell. But in case you have any interest in the matter, you will place me under further obligations by telling them most distinctly, that if they bring the china in question to my hotel by twelve o'clock to-morrow, I will give them 40l.; if the clock strikes the quarter-past, and no one appears, I shall instantly lay the whole matter before the English minister, demanding compensation for being forcibly detained, and the punishment of its authors." And taking off my hat, I wished his excellency good-morning.

As the hour of twelve sounded throughout the city, on the following day, the box and its contents, in perfect preservation, was placed in my room. I paid a thousand francs, and on the same night it formed a portion of my belongings *en route* to Páris. With a cup in my pocket I visited Sèvres, where I ascertained that this beautiful specimen of modern Sèvres had been sent by the King Louis Philippe as a present to her most Catholic Majesty of Spain on her marriage. Of course I have here only given an outline of the facts as they occurred; and having no desire to injure or question the honesty of others, I will endeavour to forget all the curious details of the affair since come to my knowledge, save that if I became the possessor of a beautiful Sèvres *déjeûner*, I did so by fair means and payment, and at considerable personal discomfort.

There is now very little to be done by the bric-à-brac hunter in Madrid; and yet there surely must be some magnificent specimens of Bueno Retiro and other specimens of Spanish china scattered about the principal towns and cities of Spain in private houses, though it has never yet been my good fortune to meet with any. In the Queen's Palace at La Granja, the whole sides of a boudoir are decorated with "Bueno Retiro" china; and I am convinced that a run through the interior of Spain would repay the bric-à-brac hunter. Of historical swords, the finest collection in the world may be seen in the Armoria at Madrid, many of them having mottoes similar to the one I have quoted in a previous page, indicative of the fine old cavalier spirit which once existed in Spain, and which I am not prepared to say does not still exist.

With all its drawbacks, Madrid during the cool season is by no means an unenjoyable *séjour* for a brief period, notwithstanding the proofs of a certain disregard of the comforts and decencies of life, laxity of police rule and discipline everywhere distinguished. But these are only " Cosas di Espagna."

The three faces of the clock over the Home Office at the Puerta del Sol hardly ever agree as to the hour. This phenomenon may be fairly taken as an emblem of the whole political, social, and moral condition of the country. Alas, poor Spain ! with all your natural charms, you possess many vices and innumerable humbugs. Should you fall, which is not improbable or impossible—for the glass of your prosperity sinks fast—I trust in the scramble some of your "Bueno Retiro" china may fall into my hands ; I will be careful that it is not broken.

QUEST VI.

ST. PETERSBURG.

I CANNOT say that I sat me down on the banks of the Neva and wept. With my pipe in my mouth I reclined in an easy arm-chair on a balcony which overlooked that wide and flowing river, and pictured to my mind what it must be in midwinter, when that blue and rushing expanse of water is converted into a broad and ice-bound high-road; in which state it has been my lot so very many times since to behold it. And here permit me to remark that every chapter of my bric-à-brac wanderings is written in the actual place, often on the very spot of which I speak.

There was a time, which appears but yesterday, so few the years—I might say the months—which have elapsed, when he who desired to visit the city of the Czars had occasion to brace up his nerves and to call alike on his physical powers and his patience; for the journey by land from the Prussian frontier,

whether in midsummer or in midwinter, was one of
intolerable fatigue and discomfort, the only choice of
evils being between death from intense cold, and
suffocation from intense heat, without one spot of
interest or beauty to vary the monotony of the way.
If railway travelling, however, be not to the majority,
as it is to me, more fatiguing than posting, matters
are greatly improved ; for justice and truth compel
me to admit that Russian railways, if they are slow
and constantly on the halt—more for the benefit of
the owners of the buffets than the convenience or
gastronomic indulgence of travellers—are replete
with comfort—more so, indeed, than those of any
other nation in which it has been my good or evil
fortune to journey. But here we are in that vast
capital, where the magnificent statue of its founder,
the great Peter, turns his horse's tail towards the
colossal gilded dome of St. Isaac's, a mighty edifice,
built, at the cost of millions, on a foundation of piles,
which the public voice declares already to be sinking.
However, as regards Petersburg and its palaces and
museums and monasteries, I must refer my readers
to other pages ; I invite them to take a walk, pro-
vided they are in good physical condition, in search

of bric-à-brac. The exchange, an event of rare occurrence, is at nine roubles the pound sterling at the moment I write these lines; so that, spite of the absurd price generally asked for articles, good, bad, and indifferent, we may chance to make a few good bargains.

Ten years since, in the days when Russian railways were not, and upsets in snowstorms were as common as telegrams, the capital of All the Russias was—I mean no pun—a capital place for bric-à-brac; and here and there is still to be found much that is worthy of the collector's researches. But, alas, at St. Petersburg, as elsewhere, that which might once have been secured for a rouble is now difficult to obtain for a pound. I suggest to the connoisseur who first visits the city of the Czars to select some friend, if he has one, who speaks the language—in default of a friend, pay an interpreter—and then drive to the porcelain manufactory, situated about four versts (or three miles) from the city. I do not say the drive is a pleasant one, far from it; but without trouble, and the exercise of patience and endurance, there is seldom much to be gained. So submit cheerfully to be bumped for two versts over an ill-paved city, and to be rebumped for two more over the vilest of roads. Even should you require a sheet of diachylon plaster on your return, you will neither regret the pain nor the outlay.

The manufactory in question, which commenced under the auspices of Catharine, has existed for more than a century, and is still under the protection of the empire. In other days, previous to the reduction of duties on foreign importations, which now fill the market, it did a thriving home trade. Even now, I cannot speak too highly either of the workmen or of the work produced in the factory. True, there is little originality of taste or design; but the copies, particularly those of figures and groups, taken from models of Dresden, Berlin, and elsewhere, are equal to, and in some measure more accurate and life-like, as well as more delicate in outline and effect, than those produced in later days either at Meissen or the royal manufactory of the latter city, and infinitely cheaper. For the most part they are uncoloured; but the glaze is very clear and smooth; and I have been fortunate enough to obtain some specimens worthy of, and equal to, any of the productions in Europe. The painting—generally, I fancy, the work

of German artists—is equally beautiful; and some
vases and *déjeûners* sent to the Exhibitions of 1851
and 1862 in England, and which were unfortunately
returned in some measure broken, were magnificent
specimens of the ceramic art. A little more originality—figures and forms possessing more nationality
of character—is all that is wanting to enable the
produce of the Russian imperial factory to vie with
the ceramic *chefs-d'œuvre* of present and past ages.

There are few of what may be fairly termed bric-
à-brac shops in Petersburg,—in fact, the only two I
know of, where *objets d'art*, as they are termed, may
be found, and to which I can recommend a visit with
the hope of any successful result, are those of
Messrs. Negri and G. Tognolati; the former on the
Nevsky Prospect, the latter at No. 39, Kamenney
Ostrowskey Prospect. Mr. Negri is a most obliging,
agreeable person to deal with; and I must do him
the justice to say that I have on more than one
occasion purchased from him some exquisite Wedgwood medallions, as also some small but choice
specimens of Sèvres, Vienna, and Berlin china, at a
very reasonable outlay. Mr. Tognolati, an Italian,—
who has recently left the city for what may be

termed the immediate environs, and combines his dealings in *objets d'art* with the fabrication of macaroni, in both of which pursuits, to all appearance, he is successful,—has also occasionally some fine specimens of carved furniture, and is always ready and obliging in showing what he has to the stranger, even should no purchases be made. He looks for rather higher gains than Mr. Negri. A packet of paper roubles will not go far with either gentleman, however.

But though Negri's and Tognolati's are the only bric-à-brac shops of which I have any practical knowledge, there is a vast field for the hunter alike in Petersburg and Moscow; though it has never as yet been my good fortune to visit the latter city. But in order to avoid the beaten track of dealers, it is necessary to get introductions to private houses in company with some one who knows the language well. In such cases your hunting-field is full, or rather was full, of game; and courtesy of manner, combined with attention, may then enable you, without offence, to be a purchaser, though the seller be not exactly a dealer. In this manner, some years since, I became the possessor of two of the finest

Wedgwood vases of their kind I have ever seen, and which, being then in my apprenticeship, I subsequently sold for about a sixth of their worth to a friend who had a valuable collection of that beautiful ware. This was one of the lessons I learnt: from that time a Wedgwood vase has risen a hundred per cent. in my estimation. It is almost inconceivable what a vast quantity of Wedgwood found its way to the city of the Czars. Doubtless very much still remains, if it could be discovered, though much of it may not exactly be for sale. Sèvres however, of the finest quality and period, Dresden and Berlin and Viennese porcelain, still remains in great quantities. The palaces are full of it. The museum has some lovely specimens; and the active and energetic hunters, with time, means, and experience, still do so much, that I believe the first-class dealers of Bond Street, such as Messrs. Joseph, Davis, and others, are wont to endure a journey to St. Petersburg, if not annually, at no very long intervals, in search of treasures; and, if report speak truly, they never return without some valuable acquisitions both from the capital and from Moscow.

I possess the adventurous hunter-spirit, and always

decide on chasing my game home wherever to be
found, whether in the woods and broadlands of my
fatherland, or on foreign shores. In like manner, I
never allow a chance to escape me when in search of
bric-à-brac, always bearing in mind that, whether
in the humblest shop or in the most magnificent
repository of *objets d'art*, something may be discovered, ofttimes more successfully in the former
than the latter. On these grounds I unhesitatingly
accepted the suggestion of a friend who proposed to
take me to the private residence of a Circassian lady,
who had a small but choice collection which she was
courteous enough to show to her friends, and with
which, of course, she had no desire to part. Nevertheless, like all other collectors, after some trifling
fencing and interchanging of courtesies, it appeared
that she had no objection to dispose of her treasures
in a dear market, she having purchased them in a
cheap one. Introductions over, a glance around the
room—which was sufficiently spacious, but, like most
Russian houses, lightly furnished, with here and
there a gorgeous highly-gilded arm-chair or sofa, and
with little apparent comfort—I cast my longing eyes
on some ceramic treasures with which a cabinet was

filled, and we commenced business. Meanwhile I
had truly been informed that my hostess was not a
dealer. Looking on her with a practical eye, her portrait may be thus drawn: age about seventy; rather
sharp and prominent features; the remnant of what
might have been teeth; a tongue which surpassed any
tongue (pardon me, ladies!) that I had ever previously
listened to, so excessive was its volubility. The
weather was hot, and her costume appeared to me to
consist simply of a somewhat dirty cotton dressing-
gown. How was I, then, a stranger in Russia, seek-
ing to secure some of her Sèvres cups, to know with
whom I had the honour of discussing the merits
and value of her ceramic treasures? So, silently, I
examined and appraised those set before my longing
eyes, wondering how the lady, as I had been told
she was, should have had such good taste and knowledge as to gather them together, and such bad taste
as to present herself in that dirty and discoloured
dress in the presence of visitors. Here and there I
selected some choice specimen which I was desirous
to purchase, but which, for the most part, she de-
clined to sell. At length, wearied by her continued
refusals and constant chatter, I seized on two charm-

ing cups, and, without further comment, placed golden sovereigns by their side. She clutched the coins, and I thought the battle won; but then appealing to my companion in the Russian tongue (unknown to me) she replaced the money on the table. "You must give another half-sovereign," said he, smiling. Anxious to have the treasures, which were really very beautiful, I gave the required addition, and forthwith the sovereigns descended to some hidden pocket in the cotton dressing-gown. The cups were mine. My friend also obtained a cup; and after innumerable shakings of hands, bows, and adieux, we parted, not without expressions on the lady's part to the effect that she hoped we should repeat our visit at some future time.

No sooner were we on our drosky than my companion burst into fits of laughter.

"What's the joke?" I inquired.

"Joke? Why, your consummate coolness with the old lady!"

"Lady?" I replied.

"Yes," said he; "a Circassian princess; and her son, who was so anxious to sell that vase which she refused, a Circassian prince."

"Well," said I, "we parted on the most amicable
terms, and, princess or no princess, she is the hardest
hand at a bargain, and has the most lively tongue, I
ever had the honour to encounter."

I have sketched this little matutinal farce simply
to remark that there are a variety of Circassian or
other princesses in Petersburg equally desirous of
fair barter; and, time and opportunity presenting
themselves, I have no doubt that the field for the
bric-à-brac hunter is vast and full of treasures.

But there is another and most interesting locale
to which I have not yet alluded. I must describe it
in detail. It is termed "Vshyvio-Rynok," or, in
plain English, the Louse Market. During the year
1862 the whole of this immense market was destroyed by fire. The tremendous conflagration may
be readily conceived when I state that the place was
entirely composed of wooden buildings, for the most
part filled with combustible matter, ranging from
valuable pictures and furniture to old rags, tar, oil, and
pitch. The fire commenced at 4 P.M., and was burning
till the midday following. During this tremendous
fire property of all kinds was ruthlessly cast into
a canal; thus books, china, pictures, silk, eastern

shawls, and objects of untold value, were destroyed and lost for ever ; and what had been one of the richest and most interesting places of the city was in a few hours converted into one vast smoking heap of ashes. It was, indeed, a perfect wreck. Here and there casks of nails, pots, pans, and copper zamovars, or Russian tea-urns, were all melted up together ; in another part, where crockery and china merchants had exhibited their wares, plates and dishes by the dozen were consumed *en masse*, so intense was the heat. A portion of one dozen I have now in my possession. It was, indeed, a sad scene of ruin and destruction. Scarcely anything was saved. Splendid Sèvres, Dresden, clocks of great value, and bric-à-brac collected for years in every mart in Europe and the East, jewels, Cashmere shawls, Lyons silk—all one heap of ashes.

The original market—which was as old as the city —was, in fact, simply a bazaar of great extent, in which were exhibited for sale articles from the world at large, and in which every purchaser, from the highest to the lowest, could suit himself on reasonable terms.

Although much fair dealing doubtless takes place

there, I will by no means answer for the fortunes that were and are dishonestly made. In Russia it is possible that stolen goods may be received from a thief with impunity. At all events I have witnessed the purchase by a dealer of a choice article of china for a few roubles, which I have almost immediately secured for double the sum paid, with the knowledge that I still became the owner cheaply. It was not for me to inquire from whence or whither it came, but the appearance of the vendor, who gladly received the trifle given for it, convinced me it was no heirloom.

Hours have I passed with much interest and amusement in the old as the modern market, bracing my nerves against the severity of a Russian winter's day, or overcome by the heat of summer, but when does the keen hunter give up his game whatsoever may be the elements he has to contend with? And as regards these markets or bazaars, if such they may be called, there is little difference, save that articles of real value day by day become more scarce, and their price greatly augmented both to buyer and seller. No doubt but that many precious objects of Sèvres, Wedgwood, Dresden, and Vienna porcelain, of unmistakeable beauty and age, and bearing pure marks, still find their way into the dealers' hands for a few roubles, and are sold for hundreds; how obtained, I will not venture to assert; and neither the buyers nor the sellers give themselves any trouble to ascertain. However, the old saying, "I got this or that for nothing," is no longer heard; and whenever a beautiful unbroken group, or a rare cup and saucer is met with, lucky the hunter who obtains it at any reasonable price. There was a time not long ago, say about the year 1854, when I had the good fortune to become the possessor of two Wedgwood vases of extreme beauty, and several plaques of unrivalled chasteness, for a price for which scarcely one, even if found, could now be purchased. My knowledge of the value of these lovely specimens was then very far from being that which experience and constant practice has since given.

I will close these recollections of my hunting days in the city of the Czars with a trifling anecdote, only indirectly connected with Petersburg, it is true, but which will not be without interest to those for whom these pages are more particularly written.

Being in Naples many years since, among numerous other articles of bric-à-brac, I became the possessor of a specimen, which, though greatly in doubt, I had much reason to believe was a Palissy dish. My belief in its genuineness arose from the fact of its great similarity to a dish I had previously seen in a first rate collection, and from my knowledge of its having been many years in the possession of a highly respectable Neapolitan family; on the other hand, doubts were suggested to my mind by its extreme beauty and brightness of colouring, the remarkable clearness and admirable representation of the shell fish, and fern flowers with which it was adorned, and by the delicacy of its outline, which is not always characteristic of the old specimens of that remarkable labourer in the field of ceramic art. Moreover, the price for which I obtained it was about the tenth part of its value if it had really been formed by the artistic hands of Palissy. It was very beautiful, however, in any case, and with care and pride, I carried it to my cottage home in England.

By very many it was admired, and though doubtful of its genuineness, I day by day looked on it with increasing delight. But alas,—as is, and

always will be the case with collectors, who are ever
and anon doomed to see the illusions which have
gathered about some of their treasures entirely
destroyed,—I showed my dish to various connoisseurs
of ceramic art, and one and all pronounced it beautiful, but of modern French production. I was not
then aware of the fact that, for half a century, France
had produced such works as copies from Palissy.
Very charming these copies were, and numberless
specimens are still to be had.

The charm, however, was broken, not so much
because my dish—with its beautiful and almost
living fish in the centre, its crabs almost crawling
amidst the fern leaves on its rim, while the snails and
the mussels looked as if recently gathered from the
shore—was of less value; but because the ridiculous
pride, which all collectors more or less feel—of knowing better than their neighbours—was utterly dispelled. So one morning, when a "pleasant friend"
looked in, I decided that my dish and I should part
company.

"I have come to look at your Palissy dish," said
my friend, somewhat confident, as I thought, in his
superior knowledge. Thus he delivered his opinion.

"Oh! ah, yes; very fine specimen indeed—of French pottery; admirably executed, but as for being genuine Palissy, it is no more Palissy than I am. Sell it. You go to Petersburg, take it there, you will get double what you will in England."

Certainly he was not Palissy either in character or humility, if we can judge from history as regards that highly gifted Christian; and I did, I confess it, at the moment feel inclined to throw the dish at his head.

But reason and good humour came to my aid, and having with some bitterness replied, "No, you are certainly not Palissy," I offered him some luncheon, and the sight of a beautiful Wedgwood plaque, which I had purchased of Mr. Negri, of Petersburg, of both of which he approved, and ere he parted, I agreed to take my heretofore much prized dish to that imperial city.

It was in the days of posting from the Prussian frontier—I should rather say sledging, the season being midwinter, for the railway was not then working. In the hurry of starting, not having been able to superintend the careful packing of my dish, I found, on arriving at the end of my journey, that it was smashed into twenty pieces. The sight overwhelmed me; here, as I supposed, was the end of my treasure. Not a bit of it. I was about to cast the fragments into the rushing waters of the Neva; when a good Samaritan in female attire, my hostess, entered my room with a note requesting my attendance at an ambassadorial gastronomic entertainment; hour 7, by the clock of St. Isaac.

The good lady looked at me with evident commiseration, knowing my love for such articles of vertu, and then at the broken dish. "What a pity, sir; how badly packed it must have been. Why, the fish is alive."

"Fish!" said I, "yes, boil it for dinner, if you will; but pray take the fragments from my sight, and forget that it was once a dish in which a pike might have been proud to have been served before the emperor. She gathered up the remains and departed; and a few days subsequently I also departed for old England.

"What did you do with the Palissy dish, dad?" said the heir to my Spanish château, after I had been welcomed home.

"Did, my boy, why gave it away to be sure," and the subject dropped.

About six months afterwards, duty again called me to Petersburg; the morning of my arrival was brilliant summer-time. I awoke from a lengthened slumber after the fatigue of a journey of several consecutive days and nights, sprang out of bed, and prepared for the matutinal cold bath. When behold, on the table before me, my precious dish, or a most remarkable counterpart. I wrapped my dressing-gown around me, and rang the bell. "Beg," said I to the servant, "Miss B—— to do me the favour of a few minutes' conversation." The good woman entered, smiling, hoped I had slept well, and had a good appetite for breakfast. "Both," said I, "thanks, but what about this dish: it is, as far as I can see, for as yet I have not touched it, precisely like that the fragments of which I gave you to throw into the Neva."

"It is the very same," said the good lady; "a traveller came here and mended it, and with pleasure I return it to its rightful owner. It was admirably restored."

"I will not have it again," I replied, "it is yours; but I will take it to Negri's, and try and sell it for you—I shall ask fifty roubles, cheap at the money."

I did so. Negri admired it, as all had, regretted that it had been broken, and promised to do his best to convert it into current coin of the realm, which then, as now, was dirty paper, and I left it in his safe keeping.

Months again elapsed ere I returned to the imperial city, and visited his collection. "What have you done with the dish," said I, after having purchased a few trifles he had kindly reserved for me.

"I have it still," he replied; "I could have sold it a huudred times had it not been repaired, but you limited me as to price, and I could not take less."

"Be good enough to send it to my hotel." He did so, properly packed as I supposed, and having insisted on giving my good hostess an ample equivalent, I once more took it to England. On my arrival it was again in fragments. I sent for a clever china mender, whom I had been in the habit of employing. "Can you restore that?" said I, showing him the dish.

"Certainly, sir," and he did restore it far better than it had previously been restored, and it is now after all its wanderings over thousands of miles and misfortunes, still worthy of admiration, the property

of one whom I esteem, but whose collection, although
in its infancy, or I greatly mistake, will become as
each year goes round, of far greater quality and
account, to which I shall endeavour to add ; knowing
that the "bric-à-brac" fever, once caught, is rarely
cured.

Petersburg, for the present, adieu! You can
boast of many rough charms, though I am by no
means of the opinion that the Nevsky Prospect is the
finest street in Europe.

"Look at this, sir," says a continental dealer,
particularly in Italy, ignoring Capo di Monte, which
in beauty can rival all porcelains ; "it is true old
Saxe Dresden, came from the collection of the
Marquis de Milanaro," as if the fact imported one jot
as to its reality or origin and age—but what as to its
merit or beauty? Well, I repeat, some of the groups
of figures and vases, the production of the Imperial
Factory in Russia, modern though they may be,
are equal to any they now produce at Miessen, and
superior in form and execution, if not precisely so in
contour.

With all this there is a fashion in "bric-à-brac"
hunting, as there is in female attire, though happily

that fashion is not derived from the same source ; the one being from the French *demi-monde,* the other from imagination. An Englishman, neither good-looking nor over polite, rules the cutting out of ladies' dresses in Paris at 25*l.* a dress ; and Worcester china may be the fashion, because it is difficult to obtain fine specimens. If Mr. W. charged 5*l.* for his dresses few would employ him.

QUEST VII.

BERLIN.

THE train starts. I turn my back on the city of the Czars, and fortify myself with patience and endurance, shut my eyes on nature, which is said to be, when unadorned, adorned the most. Certainly the observation does not apply to the scenery between the capital of all the Russias and the frontier city of Königsberg, where Prussian kings are crowned by the grace of God, and buried by permission of the people. In fact, there is not one single point of interest nor a single feature of beauty throughout the long weary versts which divide the empire of Russia from the kingdom of Prussia; and although the Russian railways offer much comfort, it requires no common amount of patience to endure the journey, and no common stomach to endure the means of sustenance offered by the wayside.

In good faith, the contrast between comparative barbarism and civilisation, which is manifest within the range of a mile from frontier to frontier, is so palpable, that I can only compare the sensation with that felt upon stepping on to the pier at Dover after a boisterous passage from Calais.

Well do I recollect, in times but recently gone by, after posting from Petersburg for days and nights, the frontier was at last gained—when, half frozen by the cold, or suffocated by dust and heat, according to the season—with what intense joy I rattled over the little wooden bridge that spanned the muddy ditch—for muddy ditch it is—which divides the empire of the Czars from the kingdom of Prussia, and pulled up at the little miserable Custom-house, having nothing to declare but that I was well-nigh exhausted, and unutterably pleased at the idea of ere long finding myself in that city called Königsberg, which boasts of thirty-two bastions, eight gates, and thirty churches—though I never discovered the inhabitants to be more moral than elsewhere.

As regards bric-à-brac, there is no field for the hunter in Königsberg; at least, I never discovered such. Yet I may write in error; for could I, like Asmodeus, have been permitted to uncover the roofs and peep into the domiciles of the beer-drinking and

H

sausage-eating citizens, who dare say what art-
treasures I might have found, and how readily they
might have been converted into thalers? However,
nothing did I ever discover there except a rather
elegant little cream-coloured jug from one of dear
Wedgwood's models; but when Mein Herr, who
wished to dispose of it, permitted me to examine it,
I discovered the words "Neale & Co.'s" imprinted
on the ware—and so, good-morning!

Let us now journey on to Berlin. Berlin! the
very writing of the name causes my heart to beat
and my blood to boil, and the hand which holds a
pen seems to grasp a revolver, the hilt of a Toledo
blade, or touch the trigger of a Snider. What days
of more than solitude have I passed from sunrise to
sunset in that beautiful but insupportably dull city!
How often have I paced beneath the Linden to kill
an hour, in the fear of being compelled to kill
myself! How have I longed for night, that I might
sleep till the dawn of another day; and when that
day has come, how I have longed for night again!
Not that there is no sport for the bric-à-brac hunter;
far from it, as I shall soon tell you. Moreover, the
game, if not of the very finest condition, is plentiful,

but strictly preserved,—indeed, so strictly, if of any
beauty and rarity, that a Rothschild or a millionnaire
alone has a chance of bagging any; and all I can say
is, that if the sellers thereof get the price they
demand, I heartily wish that, instead of being a
hunter, I were a seller.

It happened that I found myself in No. 16, first-
floor back, Hôtel d'Angleterre, Berlin, having been
there previously about thirty times, at the very
period when the army of needlegun renown were
marching to glory—that is to say, to have their own
heads broken, with an ardent desire to break those
of their enemies—in other words, on the eve of those
untoward events for Austria called Sadowa and
Königgrätz, which changed the Berliner Somniferoso
into the Berliner Bombastioso.

Truly these were exciting times for the beautiful
sleepy city of the Linden-avenue. The betting at
the twenty-groschen-per-head table-d'hôte was at or
about five to four, with no takers, that Benedek
would sleep in the royal palace in the Schloss Platz
within a fortnight. Under these circumstances, I
rose one morning early and went forth into the city
—the contrast of whose beauty and architectural

magnificence with the condition of the inhabitants is
most striking—in search of bric-à-brac, hugging to
my heart of hearts the innocent belief that some
slight fear of coming pillage might, from all I had
heard on the previous evening, have entered into the
minds of the dealers in what are ofttimes incorrectly
termed works of art, suggesting to them that it
might be better to sell cheap than suffer utter loss
from pillage or destruction. It was an ignoble,
ungenerous, selfish idea, no doubt; but the desire to
become the possessor, cheaply, of some exquisite
Berlin groups, vases, &c., or for nothing, according to
the usual phraseology—which means half their value
—was an influence too strong to be combated.

I tripped jauntily up the Linden with fond
anticipations of my wishes being realised, the more
so as I had practical proof of the apparent need of
the inhabitants : for as I gazed up the street on that
which appeared to be the habitation of a prince, a
window suddenly opened in the lower story, and a
cobbler hung out a pair of boots for sale; on the
second story a tailor had done the same by a waist-
coat and breeches ; and on the top floor, probably
the fifth, a woman, performing the matutinal offices,

cast into the street a shovel of potato-peelings on the heads of the passers-by. A few steps farther, near a building apparently a palace, an Israelite saluted me from an attic, asking if I had anything to exchange; while below I observed linen hanging out to dry, which belonged, doubtless, to a gallant officer who was being shaved by the barber hard by in a cave below the pavement.

Now writing as I do these perfectly true little historiettes of my bric-à-brac hunting throughout Europe, I find it necessary thus to introduce them to the several cities and shops where my wandering footsteps may have led me. My opinions as regards places and people, are my opinions, nothing more. Let others judge for themselves; and therefore having done and seen all that Murray tells you to do and see—not that he is always correct—put on your hat, handle your umbrella, if you have one, and let us walk abroad; always bearing in mind that the fact of being asked ten thalers for a Berlin cup, and fifty for a Berlin group, by no means implies that you are to give it—certainly not. Offer that which your judgment and taste—if you possess either—dictate; or do as I have done, though your purse may be far

better filled: give, without you are determined to
have the treasure on which you have set your heart
at any price, just thirty per cent. below that which
experience tells you the object to be actually worth.
I say this to the novice, not to the connoisseur, for
he knows, and knows well, how to act—at least he
believes he does.

There are many bric-à-brac shops at Berlin. Herr
Lewy, or Levy, or, if you will, Levi—for he is an
unquestionable Israelite, as, indeed, nearly all bric-à-
brac dealers are—is the first to whom I should
recommend a visit. Like all dealers, he seeks his
price, and a tolerably heavy one it is; but he is fair
and truthful, and, moreover, a first-rate judge ; and
at times he has many articles worthy of admiration.
In fact, he is first and foremost, in my humble
estimation, as a Berlin dealer. His address is
Dorotheen-strasse, No. 20.

Herr Meier, No. 2 Grenzhaus—commonly called
the English Parliament—has by far the largest
collection in Berlin—a splendid selection of Venetian
glass, and a great variety of carvings and china
worthy of the collector's notice. Unless that collector, however, has a very long purse, or intends to

purchase at the price desired by Herr Meier, it is as well he should avoid the sin of temptation, and that of coveting what he cannot obtain.

There are also Herr Arnold, No. 26 on the Linden, and Herr Frescati, No. 21. In the shops of these two gentlemen may sometimes be found rare art-treasures. Happy he who can afford to give the prices asked for them.

Herr Leuschner has also a bric-à-brac shop in Tannen-strasse, No. 15. Formerly he had a modest collection in a shop on the Linden; but I have invariably found, and practically proved the fact in many foreign capitals, that bric-à-brac sellers rise rapidly as regards fortune.

Although the foundation of the celebrated porcelain manufactory and museum of Berlin is to be attributed to the great monarch, statesman, poet, and philosopher, Frederick the Great of Prussia, who, in the midst of the mighty wars in which he was engaged, turned his attention to the beautiful fabric which was beginning to attract the lovers of the fine arts, there had been made in Berlin thirteen years previously (1750), under the immediate direction of Wilhelm Caspar Wegel, a first attempt to

produce specimens of the ceramic art. Wegel
pretended that he was in possession of certain
secrets, and continued to carry on his business for
seven years. Some of his works are even now to be
met with; the cipher at the bottom (W) is still to
be found. The pieces are well formed, with
good colour, exhibiting fair workmanship, painting,
glazing, and rich gilding.

In 1761, John Ernest Gotzkowski the younger
commenced a new manufactory in the Leipziger-
strasse. He obtained the secret of porcelain fabric
from Ernest Heinrich Richard, who had been
employed in Wegel's establishment, and, having
analysed the products, had made considerable progress. For the communication of his secrets Gotzkowski gave Richard 4000 dollars, and for a salary
of 1200 dollars Richard undertook the direction.
The celebrated enamel-painter Jacque Claude, and
Elias Meyer the plastic modeller, from Meissen, with
other workmen from that town, joined the establishment. Gotzkowski did not personally pursue his
undertaking, but placed it under the management
of the commissioner Grunenger, which led to his
employment, from the year 1763 to 1786, as the

head of the royal porcelain manufactory at Berlin. During the Seven Years' War, King Frederick had an opportunity of noticing the manufactories at Dresden and at Meissen. He induced the best workmen, painters and modellers, among whom were Meyer, Kleppel, and Bohme, to accompany him to Berlin; and with their assistance, and at his own expense, enriched his metropolis with the important and beautiful porcelain fabric since celebrated throughout Europe. Grunenger had soon to congratulate the king on the further addition of men of talent and celebrity, and Frederick the Great liberally endowed the newly-founded institution. Meyer received an annuity of 1500 dollars, Kleppel 1100, and Bohme 1000.

Grunenger has given an account of his labours to obtain men best adapted for the different departments of the porcelain manufactory, among them Richard Bowman, and others of some note. From the year 1763 must be dated the actual foundation of the royal establishment; for then Gotzkowski, in the month of August, gave up to the king the whole of his fabric of porcelain, receiving 225,000 dollars, and entering into a contract for the sale of his

secrets. From the specification and inventory drawn
up on the occasion, some idea may be formed of the
magnitude of his enterprise. There were 7 administrators, 1 artist, 1 model-master, 2 picture-inspectors,
6 furnace-men, 3 glaze-workers, 5 lathe-turners,
3 potters, 6 mill-workers, 2 polishers, 6 sculptors,
6 embossers, 6 founders, 11 designers, 6 earthenware-
moulders, 13 potter-wheel-workers, 3 model-joiners,
1 girdler, 22 porcelain-painters, 22 picture-colourers,
3 colour-makers, 4 packers and attendants, 8 wood-
framers; making altogether 147 persons. The
attendant expenses were 10,200 dollars. It is calculated that 29,516 red and coloured earthenware, more
than 10,000 white vessels, and 4866 painted porcelain—many of them of grotesque form, and many of
the fashion of the day—were fabricated; articles
of every description—vases, flacons, groups of various
descriptions, statuary, snuff-boxes, fancy articles, ear-
rings, lamps, and everything that the artist could
suggest and the potter carry out. It is satisfactory to
know that there exist at the present day 133 models
from which these articles were fabricated; and the
results of the labour, the energy, and the taste brought
into play a hundred years ago may easily be studied.

The contract of Gotzkowski appears to have been most advantageous to him, and to have excited considerable discussion : he, however, gave up his establishment on terms that in these days would appear hardly sufficient for the payment of his many years of labour. It was in September 1763 that Frederick the Great appeared for the first time in his manufactory. His reception was, of course, worthy of the monarch, and he seems to have examined everything with the attention of a master and of an artist. His eye fell upon every object of interest, and he freely expressed his opinion. In the moulding-room and the turners' department he remained a long time, and examined the materials. Near the ovens he entered into a long conversation with one of the furnace-men, and he also discoursed freely and at length with Grunenger, who has recorded in his chronicle the sensible remarks made by his Majesty, who pointed out the improvements which he considered might be made. The questions he asked were evidently those of an individual who was conversant with his subject, and determined to pursue it. He remained about two hours, and, on retiring, promised his gracious protection to his

artists. Commissioner Grunenger, Maritius Jacobi,
Nogel, Eichman, Richard, Meyer, Clauce, Bohme and
Kleppel continued at the head of the establishment,
and directed the different departments. A sum of
140,000 dollars was devoted to the improvement of
the fabric.

Every effort was made to produce porcelain as
remarkable for its material as for its beauty. In
order to promote its introduction largely into commerce, a certain number of Jews were privileged to
purchase articles as soon as they appeared, and to
distribute them in foreign countries. This permission has formed the groundwork of Miss Edge-
worth's celebrated novel, *The Prussian Vase*. In
1769 an order was published permitting a lottery
company to purchase annually to the amount of
90,000 dollars. In September 1763 the king
appeared at the board of directors, read their report,
and ordered the construction of two edifices—one of
three stories, 350 feet in length ; the other two
stories, of 180 feet. He built a new mill for pul-
verising the materials, with apparatus for cleansing
and preparing the clay employed. He was anxious
to have, as soon as possible, new specimens. He

ordered that potter's-clay and earthy materials should be sent from all parts of his dominions, and enumerated several localities in which he himself had seen earth adapted for porcelain. The king's orders were quickly obeyed. In 1771, in the neighbourhood of Brackwitz, not far from Halle, a superior clay was discovered, from which a porcelain of exquisite beauty and whiteness was obtained, to the great delight of the monarch. Somewhat later, discoveries were made at Beerdersee and at Morland Seumwitz of earthy material of the highest quality, sufficient for consumption during a century ; and from thence the royal manufactory at this day derives its most valuable material. The reputation of the fabric was quickly extended far and near. The Duke of Brunswick and the Landgrave of Hesse-Cassel came to witness the progress ; and the Count Woronzoff, with several of the Russian nobility, were also attracted. His highness the Turkish ambassador, Achmet Effendi, a great amateur of porcelain and fully conversant with its manufacture, visited the royal manufactory, much to the satisfaction of Grunenger, who has narrated the circumstances attendant upon the visit.

The untiring zeal and energy of the king awakened a spirit of enthusiasm in every department, which led to the happiest results. Science and art were called in to superintend all the arrangements: mineralogists studied the materials, engineers constructed the ovens, chemists produced the colours, and painters composed the designs. The style and taste of the Berlin porcelain called forth the admiration of Europe; crowned heads were eager to receive presents from the royal owner; the saloons of the aristocratic world could not be considered richly furnished unless some specimen of the Prussian manufacture was exhibited. Nor was this without cause; for the beautifully enamelled surface displayed subjects after Watteau, Boucher, Savaret, Buffles; the customs of all ages; flowers, birds, insects,—exquisitely painted in colours of radiant splendour. The articles were modelled after classic forms, or according to the principles of beauty generally admitted at the period; the ornaments and the decorations were of the richest character; allegorical figures, statues from the antique, sheep, shepherdesses, and the most *rococo* as well as humorous subjects, were rapidly executed. His Majesty was perfectly de-

lighted when snuff-boxes were produced the covers
of which exhibited to his admiring courtiers miniatures of the royal personage himself; and happy was
the individual who received from such hands a mark
of royal regard. After a night broken by the agonies
of gout in his hands and feet, at six in the morning
would Frederick receive with delight the director of
the royal manufactory, who came to show a new
chef-d'œuvre, which he would place on a table by the
royal bedside. The death of the monarch did not
diminish the importance of the great establishment.
Prince Henry and Princess Amelia had already
evinced a deep interest in the ceramic art. In 1787
Frederick William II. appointed a commission,
under the direction of the minister Von Stemitz
and Count Reden, and great improvements in the
management were carried out. The same taste and
industry were everywhere encouraged. The construction of the ovens was more scientifically attended
to, in consequence of the studies of caloric and of
temperature having led to economy of fuel and regu-
lation of heat. Germany was compelled to ac-
knowledge that the perfection of porcelain had been
reached at Berlin, notwithstanding the rivalry of

Dresden, of Meissen, and of other rich cities. Since the year 1832, up to the present period, the manufactory has not ceased to deserve the admiration of the public. Colossal vases have been produced which have entered into the collections of the Emperor of Russia and the Queen of England. Probably the most beautiful are those now in the Louvre, presented to Louis Philippe in 1844. They are more than six feet in height, in the shape of amphoræ, with garlands of flowers upon a red ground, richly gilt and ornamented. In 1845 Prince Albert became possessor of a magnificent dish, two feet and a half in diameter, which he considered the *chef-d'œuvre* of the Berlin manufactory. There is no cessation of activity and emulation at the present hour, and the royal patronage is still bestowed upon the establishment.

QUEST VIII.

DRESDEN.

FROM Berlin to Dresden is a question of three or four hours' patience, an indifferent railway carriage, and four or five thalers of expenditure, considerable smoking, and as long a sleep as possible.

I say patience, inasmuch as the country through which the traveller passes, is utterly devoid of interest till the fair city is in sight, for the most part being through vast sandy though tolerably well-cultivated places, interminable pine forests, and endless halts at small stations, wherein more bad beer is imbibed, and more sausages consumed by Prussian passengers than would feed a regiment; although foreigners for the most part consider it an established fact that Englishmen monopolise that most valuable acquisition to health and gastronomic enjoyment, a good appetite; whereas nine out of every ten subjects of his Prussian Majesty, would beat the best feeder among us by a beefsteak and

I

onions, to say nothing of swallowing half his knife into the bargain.

Moreover, although four or five hours are frittered away in the transit from the city of Berlin to that of Dresden, in a train, evidently by error termed an express train, the journey might be readily accomplished, and would be so either in England or France, in two; but these German, or rather let me call them Prussian trains, are proverbially slow and sleepy, if safe.

Dresden is, or at least ought to be, the city *par excellence* for a bric-à-brac hunter. The very name of Dresden seems to convey to the senses of the lover of ceramic art all that is charming, ancient, rare, and beautiful in form and colour. Vases and groups, clocks and candelabras, excite the imagination, and fill with keen anticipation of delight the breast of an eager hunter, who, for the first time in his life approached, ere Prussian rule commenced, that still pleasant though less stirring city watered by the Elbe.

On the first night of his arrival there, rest is denied to him: his nerves are excited, his imagination conjures up the treasures he will behold on the morrow: if he sleeps at all, it is to dream of Böttcher Marcolini, Horold, and the factory at Meissen.

When I first had the good fortune, years lang syne, to visit Dresden, it was not only one of the pleasantest, but, for society, cheapness of living, comfort, and beauty, second to hardly any city in Europe. Diplomats of all nations mixed together in friendly and hospitable association, and passing visitors from foreign lands, properly accredited, were received not only by the residents in the country, but the society which had gathered together for various reasons,— such as the education of their children, economy, or a life of quiet ease, surrounded by beauties of nature, and simple elegance of daily life, in connection with health and various other attributes,—with that frank kindness which makes the world we live in, if not one of unalloyed happiness, still of passing comfort and enjoyment.

I do not presume to say that the grasping hand of territorial aggrandizement, or bigotry, or conquest, or policy, or by whatever name or words plain speaking men judge fit to use, has in any manner altered the beauties great which nature and nature's God have awarded to this favoured district; but I do say, without fear of contradiction, that the Dresden that was, and the Dresden that is, are, as far as a residence or even a temporary visit is concerned, apparently wide apart.

The object of my first journey to that pleasant abode of Saxon monarchy and art-treasures, was twofold: a brief repose from the hard, practical duties of an active life, combined with an ardent desire to examine the ceramic collections, gathered together in its museums, and not without a hope of visiting the far-famed china manufactory at Meissen, where in the days we live, hours of enjoyment to the lover of bric-à-brac may be secured, Meissen being easily gained by steam-boat on the Elbe, or by railway : the waters of the Elbe in summer decidedly for choice.

Meanwhile, as is doubtless the case with all lovers and collectors of ceramic treasures, I had heard and read, and pondered over with interest all the facts, historiettes, and anecdotes connected with what is supposed to be the first European factory of porcelain, established at Meissen near Dresden in the beginning of the 18th century. I had read how John Frederick Böttcher, an apothecary's assistant, being suspected of alchemy, had fled from Berlin, his native city, to avoid prosecution, and had taken refuge in the pleasant city of Dresden. How Augustus the Elector, the then proud and despotic ruler of Saxony, after hearing the fugitive's tale, questioned him minutely as to his knowledge of the art of making gold—then believed in—and placed him in the royal laboratory under Tschirnhausen, who was then engaged in searching for the universal medicine. In the course of the experiments which he there carried on, a composition was unexpectedly produced, exhibiting many of the characteristics of oriental china porcelain.

His Majesty, perceiving the great importance of the discovery, immediately sent him to the castle of Albrechtsbergh at Meissen, and thence with his workmen, under an escort of cavalry, to the fortress of Königstein, where pleasantly shut up from the bright world without—that is, incarcerated for despotic gain—he pursued his artistic and chemical researches.

Ay! Herr Minton, of our dear fatherland, what say you? Should you like a year in the Tower or Newgate, the better to enable you to pursue the

glorious art in which your name stands in such
honourable prominence ?

Yet, perchance, those were some of the good old
days many are so fond of croaking about, when
kings claimed the mental slavery of their subjects,
and treated the genius of man as a source of personal profit. What a lesson is open to us in these
comparatively happy and enlightened times, as
compared with the history of ages past.

Could we be permitted occasionally to look on
kings and queens as human beings, and not, as a
talented writer once observed, "coming down upon
you in velvet and fur, with crowns on their heads,"
bedizened with useless stars and ribbons; men and
women, divided from their fellow beings, both by
position and all natural feelings ;—such persons can
possibly imagine poor Böttcher, as incarcerated for
having discovered something unknown to his neigh-
bour, yet so valuable to the German race, from
which selfish profit was first to be made. For my
part, I own to the satisfaction I should feel at
beholding a foreign potentate, getting out of his
matutinal bath, if given to that refreshing habit of
cleanliness and health—the Sultan, for example, or

the King of Königgrätz—with a rough towel in his hand, having a good appetite, and somewhat late for breakfast. I take it, I should find them, without the crown, the velvet and fur, like other men, save in position mere slaves of birth.

Thousands grumble because the best of all sovereigns prefers as much repose as is consistent with her high calling, and loves to commune with nature and her God. Let such look back to the era when sovereigns were tyrants, and the genius of a subject was converted into a source of personal riches. Were I a king, I certainly would have a rare collection of bric-à-brac, but I would rather have granted a peerage to Böttcher than a prison in a castle; and he deserved it far more than a third of the number on whom it is conferred in these days, for he created art beauties which, to the hour we live, are an immense source of commerce, and undying pleasure in possession to the world at large.

In the year 1707, Böttcher, having secured the confidence of the Elector, returned to Dresden, where he pursued his experimental art with renewed vigour and eventual success.

His first productions were simply a sort of red

stone ware, scarcely to be denominated porcelain, specimens of which may now be purchased as curiosities, if not for their beauty, in almost every capital of Europe. This he brought to some perfection, but the results were more curious than elegant as works of art. In 1709, however, he succeeded in producing his white porcelain, which was brought to such perfection in 1815, that it was generally considered to be the first European discovery of porcelain, and many are still of opinion that it has never been surpassed. The merit of the discovery of the first manufacture in Europe has been generally awarded to Dresden, in 1709. But it appears only to have been a revival, inasmuch as, in 1580, Florence produced a porcelain of durable character, now almost, if not quite, unattainable. So devoted was he to the hoped-for results of his ceramic art, that, although he was not under the necessity of burning his household goods to keep his furnace alive—as was the case with the nobler Palissy—history tells us that he sat up long nights and days watching the regularity of its heat.

How he composed his artificial paste has never been known. The discovery of the natural paste, or kaolin, which he subsequently used with such great and admirable success, was made as related in a simple tale, known doubtless to most collectors and lovers of bric-à-brac, but which I will tell here for the benefit of those who may hereafter find pleasure or profit in hunting for ceramic treasures. It runs as follows :

A rich iron master, named Schnorr, when riding over his estate at Aue, near Erzgebirge, observed that his horse's feet stuck fast in some perfectly white earth or clay. Hair powder being at the period a valuable object of commerce, it immediately occurred to him that this white earth, when dried and carefully prepared, might be a valuable substitute, while subsequent experiments justified his discernment. This powder soon became an article of general use throughout Saxony. The king's guards were powdered, their pigtails cheaply whitened ; and at length Böttcher having powdered his own wig, found it so heavy that he felt convinced the so-called powder must be earth ; and having tried it in the fire, to his great delight and untold joy, discovered that it was the very material he had long sought for in vain, that is, the true kaolin. Whereupon the Elector,

his master, commanded that his subjects' wigs should
no longer be whitened with clay; the powder was
bought up, and secretly conveyed in barrels to the
porcelain manufactory, and its exportation henceforth
strictly prohibited.   What a weight was thereby
taken from the heart of Böttcher, as doubtless the
heads of the Saxons!   What ceramic treasures were
henceforth distributed to the world at large!   I
never think of the era of this discovery but it occurs
to me that every collector and dealer in bric-à-brac
should meet annually to celebrate the feast of St.
Böttcher, a saint who does more good to mankind, I
take it, than half the saints who are fêted ; for what
pleasure, and comfort, and commerce, did this discovery not produce !   But man's merits and virtues
are, alas, too soon forgotten, and this occurred " only
one hundred and fifty years " lang syne.

At that period everything connected with the
Dresden manufactory was carried on with a degree
of secrecy, that in these days of real or comparative
liberty may well excite wonderment. The workmen were bound by the most solemn oaths, and
kept in a castle, having all the characteristics of a
prison, which they were never permitted to leave,

and into which no stranger was ever allowed to enter. *"Geheim bis ins grab"*—be secret unto death—was the motto hung up conspicuously in every workshop and department. Depressing as we may suppose such conditions to have been, the workmen pursued their labour cheerfully and successfully, and brought that which the genius of Böttcher designed more nearly to perfection than, I fear, it will ever be brought again.

Now let us cross the Elbe, over that famous stone bridge, said to be the longest and finest in Germany, built as our friends of other days tell us—and why should we doubt them?—or rather let me say, paid for, by money raised by the sale of dispensations from the Pope, for permission to eat butter and eggs during Lent; Pope's pennies, in fact. Whether true or false, that a bridge was built of butter and eggs, it has stood the test of Elbe's rapid stream for many a long year, notwithstanding the waters have been known to rise sixteen feet in four hours, when the snows of winter thaw rapidly, and large masses of floating ice crush against its arches. Strong as it is, however, the centre arch gave way in 1813 to the force of powder, having been blown up by Davoust

to make good his retreat to Leipsic. However, we
are now over it, so winter though it be, let us take up
our pleasant abode in the Hotel Belle Vue, select a
cheerful room, and take a glance at the bright moon
glittering on the Elbe, and over the valley towards
Meissen, shut the casement, for the night is chilly,
and eat our supper in comfort, without asking a
dispensation or fear of excommunication, and sleep
calmly in anticipated pleasure of the morrow.

I take it for granted that those who have so far
followed my footsteps are, for the most part, ardent
lovers of the ceramic art, in fact, bric-à-brac hunters,
and that it is therefore their especial pleasure, when
visiting the capitals of Europe, to seek the abodes of
dealers in such articles, and visit them wheresoever
they are to be found. With palaces, picture galleries,
and public sights, these pages have little or nothing
to do. Pictures can scarcely be classed as bric-à-
brac, though a journey of a thousand miles would be
well repaid to linger for one bright morning in the
Gallery of Dresden. There is, however, one museum
in which the lover of bric-à-brac, who visits the fair
city of Dresden, may feast on the beautiful productions of the china factory ; where he may gloat

on the untold treasures in the Green Vaults—
"Grüne Geirölbe." They are replete with the rarest
specimens of ancient art, and hours, nay days, may
be spent in their exploration.

Having visited the "Green Vaults," brace up your
nerves, shut out all feelings of covetous longing from
your heart, and then hasten to the Japanese Palace,
or porcelain collection, "Porzellan sammlung." If
possible, select a bright sunny morning for your first
visit, because all works of art are best seen under
such auspices. You will find sixty thousand pieces
of china grouped in eighteen apartments, the
contents of which are catalogued in five manuscript
folio volumes. In addition to a large collection,
comprising the earliest periods, as well as the finest
modern productions of native Saxon ware, you will
behold a grand display of Chinese, Japanese, Italian,
and Sèvres china; with many interesting specimens
of Böttcher's earliest attempts, and several examples
of French ware, the gift of the Emperor Napoleon I.

One set of magnificent china is said to have been
given to the Elector Augustus II., by Frederick I. of
Prussia, for a regiment of dragoons fully equipped;
and a document certifying this exchange, is said to

be among the archives of Dresden, dated Nurem-
berg, 29th April, and countersigned at Charlotten-
burgh 1st May.

Having feasted on this collection, prepare yourself
the following morning by a hearty breakfast and
—the weather being fair and bright—start for
Meissen.

The road from Dresden to Meissen runs by the
left bank of the Elbe, some short distance from it,
at the foot of a range of sloping hills covered with
vineyards, from which it is said some excellent wine
is produced. The banks are also dotted over with
villas; and I have heard the prospect compared with
the neighbourhood of Florence, whereas, the woodlands make it far more agreeable.

The factory of Meissen, as I have already re-
marked, was established by Augustus II., Elector of
Saxony. I have also alluded to the experiments of
Böttcher and Tschirnhausen, who commenced them
in 1706 with brown clay found in the neighbourhood ;
and I have further related how John Schnorr of
Erzgebirge in 1811 discovered the white clay, known
hereafter as Schonnorich messe Eide von aure, which
was sold largely at Dresden and Leipsic as hair

powder, and from which, although exhausted in 1850, the finest white china was produced.

Böttcher became director of the manufactory in 1710, and it has been again and again asserted that, up to the period of his death in 1719, white china was produced in Saxony only. This is, however, scarcely to be credited, as works were previously established both at St. Cloud, and in the Faubourg St. Antoine at Paris.

In 1720, painting and gilding of a very superior character were carried on under the superintendence of Horoldts ; and in 1731 Landers, a sculptor, superintended the modelling of groups, animals and vases; from which period up to 1756 the very best productions emanated from the Dresden factory. Angelica Kauffman was numbered among the most distinguished painters, and specimens of her painting are still occasionally met with.

In 1754, Christian Wilslom Ernst Bismark, became director, and in 1778, the King of Saxony himself personally superintended the establishment. In 1796, Marcolini was appointed director, and held the post until 1814, when Von Oppel succeeded him. In 1833 then M'Lau took his place, and the manufactory has since been styled, "Königliche Sachsische Porzellan Manufactur," in fact, the Royal Factory.

The building, which stands on a commanding position, was formerly the residence of Saxon Princes, and agreeable writers have expressed much regret that it should have been so cruelly desecrated. I confess that I have no such feelings of regret. For a century and more, it has been, and it is to be hoped will still continue to be, the source of employment for taste and talent, opening year by year the most agreeable commerce to all lovers of ceramic art. There men labour for the bread of life, surrounded by taste and beauty, and from that labour produce objects distributed throughout the world; and if so be their productions are by no means equal to those of ages past, I do not envy the man who, having passed some hours in their inspection, can turn his back thereon without admiration of that which he has seen, and learnt therefrom a lesson—yes a practical lesson, which is, and I say it not uncourteously, that modern art, with all its beauty, can bear no comparison with that of our forefathers. Those who may perchance have had the good fortune to visit the Exhibition of 1851, and those of 1862 in London, and 1867 in Paris, will I fancy agree with me that, while science, as regards machinery, marches with rapid strides, art and inventive genius, as regards the beautiful, is positively at a standstill.

Having lingered in the " Green Vaults," passed many an hour in the Porcelain Museum, enjoyed a long summer's day at Meissen, let us now walk through the city, and pay a visit to the numerous emporiums of treasures—in fact, have a good bric-à-brac hunt.

It is a pleasant pastime for those who love the pursuit—yes a very pleasant pastime—and yet I must speak the truth. I know of none wherein all human passions, for the most part evil ones, require to be kept under such strict control ; they may be thus numbered : do not covet other men's goods, " jealousy," " envy," " longing," " patience," " temper," self-control, anger, economy without meanness, and honest assertions.

These passions will all trouble you and must be met calmly, courteously, patiently, with good temper, taste and experience, and money. The last above all; if you have it not, or at least sufficient to gratify

one passion, remain at home; you will only return
with sadness and regret.

Previous to commencing our walk, however, I
would be permitted to say a word to the inexperienced in bric-à-brac hunting—it is to advise them
to banish from their minds the idea, that the being in
Dresden will enable them to secure a good specimen
of Dresden china, or, save by the merest chance, any
article of *vertu*, modern or ancient, even on "reasonable" terms.

True, there was a pleasant era in days lang syne
when the fortunate hunter might win the day. That
day abroad is over; and if he desire to obtain some
really first rate specimens at a fair price, I do not
think he need take the trouble of going further than
London.

The delusions, the falsifications, the unworthy
trickeries—to call them by their right name,
forgeries—as regards marks, paintings, mendings,
&c., are incomprehensible, and the keenest and most
experienced are taken in.

Besides a grand emporium for the sale of modern
china from the Royal Factory, what are termed
curiosity shops—that is bric-à-brac shops—abound

in Dresden; and I doubt not but that they are
known to all the Hotel commissioners, who profit
accordingly. I shall decline, therefore, to offer a
word of praise or dispraise as regards any of them;
I will merely observe, that those who charge the
most, and who lead the van as bric-à-brac sellers,
are those I should be least inclined to seek. If they
have any really good specimens, they know perfectly
well where to place them, and the bric-à-brac hunter
will not obtain them without disbursing their full
value.

Beautiful, nay exquisite on a general view, as the
modern Dresden may be said to be, in form, outline,
sharpness and colouring, it is as inferior to the old,
as a turnip to a peach; indeed some of the Russian
models are much finer, and all the modern china sold
in Dresden is most absurdly priced. It so chanced
that I found myself in that pleasant city, at the
moment of its occupation by Prussian troops, on, or
about the termination of that untoward battle, called
Königgrätz, which terminated the fate of Austria,
and caused their enemies, not without reason, to be
somewhat more vain than they usually are; and I
found the inhabitants, who, to use plain words, had

been in a terrible fright, cooling down a little, to their usual pursuits.

Ten days previously, however, there was scarce a man or woman in the city who did not fear its being ransacked by the Austrian army, and doubtless all the dealers in bric-à-brac, who had some knowledge of their country's history, recollected that Meissen was the battle field between the Austrians and Prussians in 1759, when the manufactory was plundered, and the archives destroyed ; and who could venture to assert, but that their private collections might share the same fate? And with this knowledge I sought my friends, the bric-à-brac dealers, full of hope and anticipation, that I should find the market within range of my humble means.

Now, ere I say a word further on the subject of my own doings in this matter, I can safely assure ardent lovers of bric-à-brac, who fancy that Dresden is a sure find, as we say in hunting parlance, and that having found, possession is readily and cheaply acquired, that they never were more mistaken.

Of first rate " ancient" Dresden china—pure and unbroken—there is very little to be purchased in the

city of that name, and being so fortunate as to discover here and there something really worth having,
the price is truly fabulous. Of china there is cart-
loads, and much that is beautiful, though modern ;
but for the collector and connoisseur, with a rea-
knowledge of the art treasures he loves: there is
little or nothing. False marks, modern painting on
old white china, and traps of every possible kind
to catch the unwary, abound ; but of the real, and
good, and beautiful, seek it not in Dresden : you
need, in fact, as I have before suggested, go no further
than London, where, indeed, you will find far
cheaper and far truer Dresden china.

It would be useless were I to point out to the
lover of bric-à-brac the many shops by name that
are there to be found : they are legion. He who
desires to visit them, being unacquainted with the
city, has only to apply to one of those numerous
individuals who lounge about hotels, and call themselves commissioners. They know all the best and
the worst shops; but, when visiting them, trust to
yourself, if you have any knowledge of good from
bad ; if not, satisfy yourself with what you obtain,
which, as works of art, will I fear turn out to be

worthless, or false, unless some angel of luck stand at your elbow.

At the period to which I have alluded, so great had been the fear of the Austrian army visiting the city, that all that was valuable had been packed away here, there, and everywhere, in cupboards, drawers, hampers, cellars, &c.; indeed, I witnessed one hamper of Dresden cups—at least a hundred—for each of which a Paris dealer would have asked a sovereign or more, placed away under the manger of a stable.

The fear of pillage was only then subsiding, and the dealers were beginning to redecorate their shops with cups and figures, and vases, like tulips coming up in early summer; but the fear was subsiding, and so what a week previously might, I fancy, have been bought for an old song, according to common words, was even more expensive than heretofore; with the laudable idea of receiving payment for their terror and recent slack in business: and so I got little or nothing worth having. Neither is there very much worth having save modern china in this 19th century, except from private collections; and if so be there is, there is no difficulty in selling it. And yet what lover of the ceramic art should not visit that pleasant city? Few European capitals contain a greater number of objects calculated to gratify the curiosity of an intelligent traveller; moreover, it is the residence of men of taste and talent, who contribute much to render society agreeable. The town itself is more pleasing at a distance than striking; it has neither fine streets nor imposing buildings, but its situation is charming. On quitting it for other scenes, not less fair, I would name for the benefit of the bric-à-brac hunter that, notwithstanding all the vigilance of the Elector of Saxony, one of the workmen named Stöbzel, escaped from Meissen, about the period of Böttcher's death in 1719, and reached Vienna; to which city my next chapter will introduce you in safety.

The importance of porcelain as an article of commerce was then so strongly recognised by the princes of Germany, that he was enthusiastically received. And thus, as I shall hereafter explain, arose in 1720 the great manufactory.

When Frederick attacked Dresden in 1745, the Porcelain King did not neglect to carry away his china and pictures, although he left the Electoral archives. The finest specimens at Meissen were made previous to the Seven Years' War. No expense was spared in their production—no sum refused to obtain them; while Count Brühl, minister to Augustus III., was the chief supporter of the manufactory under Taudler.

Ere I quit Dresden, I cannot refrain from relating a somewhat amusing little anecdote, told to me by a Russian gentleman—and there are few more agreeable fellow-travellers—with whom I once chanced to visit Meissen.

Among various articles of modern china which we had selected to purchase, I had chosen a good model of a pug dog.

"What are you about to do with that animal?" said the Russian.

"Do with it," I replied, "why, make it a present to a lady who is very fond of dogs, so fond, indeed, that at times they are rather a nuisance to her friends. I intend, on presenting it, to express the hope that this may be the only dog henceforth seen in her boudoir, at least when I have the pleasure of calling."

"*Parbleu!*" he exclaimed, laughing; "I can tell

you a somewhat droll story touching a 'pug-dog,' well known, I fancy, in Russia.

"Baron P—— was the owner of a very handsome one, which Catherine the Great was continually admiring, so that the Baron could do no less than present it to the Empress, who most graciously received it, and henceforth poor pug was so constantly crammed with luxuries, which he had never previously tasted, that he actually died of repletion.

"The Empress, much grieved at this event, said to one of her officers: 'Take P——, and let him be flayed and stuffed.' In obedience to this despotic order, straightway the officer went to the Baron's house, and with a face full of horror, repeated the Empress's commands.

"As may be readily conceived, the Baron by no means considered his position a pleasant one—for he well knew if she really was determined to flay and stuff him, there was no appeal. Nevertheless, he prevailed on the officer to let him go to the Empress, who, on hearing of the ridiculous mistake, was ready to expire with laughter. She soon, however, dispelled the Baron's fears, by telling him it was the dead pug, to whom she had given his name, and that she had ordered it, not him, to be flayed and stuffed.

"By the spirit of Böttcher, I verily believe the china pug you have purchased is a facsimile of the Baron."

Visit Meissen, my friends, and recollect, Art is truth : and truth is religion.

QUEST IX.

VIENNA.

WHEN the fruit-trees are in the full blossom of late spring-time, and all nature is alive, there are few pleasanter scenes than that on which the traveller looks as he journeys from Dresden, by the banks of the Elbe, to the Austrian frontier at Bodenbach. From thence to the ancient city of Prague the route is scarcely less interesting; and a few days' ramble amid the mountains of the Saxon Tyrol will amply reward all lovers of the picturesque.

Ere I commenced my quests as a bric-à-brac hunter in various capitals and towns throughout Europe, I felt, and still feel, that I might possibly create additional interest by briefly describing to my readers the countries and places in which for a time I lingered, rather than by dwelling merely on the tastes which induced such pursuits, inasmuch as to those who have not precisely the "bric-à-brac" fever, which causes me to halt at every window of

what is generally termed a curiosity-shop, some few
words in reference to the modes and manners of
those far away in foreign lands, among whom my
pursuits have led me to associate—as to the beauties
of nature which, from time to time, my wanderings
have enabled me to look upon and enjoy—must, I
imagine, cause pleasant sensations to the lover of
travel. Any man, be he who he may, who has
ears to hear and eyes to behold, who in simple language can tell his tale of other lands, and offer his
experiences for the benefit of his fellow men, must
cause pleasure to many who seek knowledge beyond
the narrow channel which divides them from people
of other tongues, tastes, and habits.

Take, for instance, the volume recently offered to
the perusal of her subjects by our gracious Queen ;
how simple the language, how truthfully and pleasant
the descriptions! Yet I would scarcely desire to call
that man a Christian, or my friend, who could read
it with a heart untouched with admiration—that in
every word he finds the woman, with all the best
feelings of human nature predominating over the
position of the queen. But I must return to the
subject of bric-à-brac.

I once heard or read of a Spanish nobleman who possessed, as Spanish grandees not seldom do possess, innumerable titles. Travelling in Navarre, this haughty hidalgo was benighted during a heavy thunder-storm, and pulled up after midnight at a small posada, the owner of which had retired to rest. After much ringing and knocking, mine host's head appeared at the window of an upper story, and he begged to be informed who was below and what they wanted. "It is the Duke of—, Marquis of—, Count of—, and so forth, grandee of Spain," replied one of the hidalgo's followers. "Well, then," said the sleepy host, "*vados ustedes con Dios,* for I have no room for so many." Such is precisely my case as regards the ancedotes which crowd on the mind of the travelling bric-à-brac hunter. So I must hasten on to Vienna.

Now, wheresoever I wander, I make it a rule to obtain all possible information from my fellow-travellers, if cognisant of their language, and again and again I have found the practice of no common value. I am fully aware that one of the most striking attributes of our national character is the reserve peculiar to Englishmen, who are in the habit, when visiting foreign lands, of intrenching themselves against every possibility of making new acquaintances with their fellow-men by any other means than the formally accredited medium of personal introduction. "I never was introduced to him," observed some one in palliation of not having rushed forward to aid a drowning stranger.

A characteristic anecdote has also been told of an Englishman, for the truth of which I can vouch. This punctilious traveller, who was no doubt impressed with that habitual idea of self-importance which we too often carry beyond the white cliffs of Albion, found himself, in the course of his continental travels, at a ball given by a British ambassadress. While pleasantly engaged in the refreshment-room a gentlemanly-looking person approached him, and expressed a hope that all his wants were well supplied, and that he was enjoying himself; to which courteous address the young "swell," so I must call him, with the sensitiveness of offended dignity, drawing himself up into an attitude of *hauteur*, replied, "Sir, you have the advantage of me!" What he thought of himself when he subsequently discovered that the kind advances he had so rudely repulsed had been offered by the ambassador himself, whose well-known courtesy and kindness to the humblest, as well as the most distinguished of his guests, was proverbial, I know not; but I would hope it taught him that the highest breeding ever shows itself in the most gentle courtesy to all.

There are upon earth no greater travellers than my fellow-countrymen. In every part of Europe and the known world they are to be met with, and yet nothing is more difficult than to convince them that there are many advantages resulting from usages and practices on the Continent which we transplant to our fatherland. My own ideas are to the last degree cosmopolitan; and as my companion in the railway was a most agreeable-looking gentleman, I at once expressed my admiration of the scenery through which we were rapidly travelling, and obtained from him in courteous words the information that we were to be fellow-passengers as far as Prague. The offer of a good Havannah, which was cordially accepted, inaugurated our acquaintance, and my agreeable fellow-traveller's society made my journey a very pleasant one. He not only gave me much information with reference to the city of

Prague, but induced me to remain there a day; and more, found out for me two bric-à-brac dealers, whose storehouses it would have been almost impossible for me to discover, inasmuch as the one lived over an Italian warehouse, and the other in the suburbs. At these emporiums I beheld much of interest, and had tolerable sport at little outlay. Prague, moreover, is a pleasant old city, full of historical reminiscences, wherein the traveller may employ himself profitably for a brief period, while there is also much to be found that will well repay the bric-à-brac hunter, blest with leisure and patience. The city is situated on the banks of the Moldan, spanned by one of the most celebrated bridges in Europe, at least seven hundred feet long, and so wide that three carriages may pass abreast. This bridge, which stands on sixteen piers, surmounted by twenty-eight statues of saints, was built by Charles IV. in 1357. Throughout Austria all bridges are adorned with a statue of Saint Nepomuc, the patron-saint of bridges, who suffered martyrdom by being cast from that at Prague by order of King Wenceslaus. The saint's offence was his refusal to reveal to his majesty the secrets of his

queen's confession. The streets of Prague are broad
and airy, the palaces not remarkable, but the people,
as at Königsberg, ought to be, if they are not, the
most moral and pious in Europe, as they have ninety-
two churches and chapels, and about forty convents,
to pray in.

The city is large, and divided into three parts by
the river, but not thickly populated. The royal
castle, which crowns a hill, commands an extensive
prospect over a fine country, and is the point for all
travellers to visit; it is surrounded by fine and well-
kept gardens.

From Prague I sped on to Vienna. The road,
save here and there, offers little of fine scenery, and
less of interest,—the country is rich and well culti-
vated,—till the battle-field of Wagram is reached ;
and then across the Danube to the fair city of Vienna,
than which there are few more agreeable. To one
who has been there lang syne, and returns after a
lapse of years, the changes that have taken place are
somewhat startling. The ramparts by which the
ancient city was surrounded are destroyed; new
broad streets and elegant houses have arisen as by
magic; public gardens, lakes, pleasant walks, and a

L

noble opera-house to crown the whole, have been conjured into being. The extensive suburbs are now, as it were, joined to the city; the ancient portion, and that which heretofore was a small and lively town, is now a grand city. The hotels are numerous, good, and not extravagant for those who desire to live reasonably. The beer, celebrated throughout Europe, has lost nothing of its excellence, and may be justly termed the most healthy beverage that manhood can imbibe. In proof of its excellence I may observe that, at one single brewery in Vienna, during six months of the year, fourteen hundred and sixty barrels of beer, each containing thirty-six gallons, are daily brewed. Even the American "corpse reviver," so much estimated by the Parisians, by no means surpasses it. To the bric-à-brac hunter Vienna also offers many charms; and there are numerous dealers of varied repute, though there, as elsewhere, the price has risen 200 per cent.; and those who a few years since lived apparently on soup, sauer-kraut, and sausages with contentment, and were satisfied with merely twenty per cent. profit, now dwell in fine houses, and display their goods in shops that would do no discredit to Regent Street or

the Rue de la Paix. Fashion, however, here as elsewhere, rules the taste as regards porcelain, or what
is termed "bric-à-brac," as it does in reference to
chignons, bonnets, and crinolines; so one day people
are mad about Chelsea ware, to-morrow distracted
on the subject of Sèvres, anon Wedgwood or Dresden,
Battersea enamel, or Capo di Monte, and so on.
Vienna china—and I am at a loss to account for the
reason—appears never to have been held in very
high estimation in England. The imperial factory
has nevertheless produced some wonderful specimens
of workmanship, especially in rich gilding, unequalled
in Europe. In the Vienna museum—recently established, as if to deplore the death of the factory—
there may be seen specimens of form, colour, and
painting, particularly as regards plates and cups,
unrivalled even at Meissen or Berlin, and unequalled
in the range of modern art. No manufactory, as I
shall explain in subsequent pages, had more difficulties to contend with at its birth; none ought to
be more regretted on its downfall. It was long ere
the precious means of producing porcelain, guarded
with such secrecy and jealousy, was obtained by
Austria, owing to the continued precautions of the

Elector of Saxony.   But, as workmen with knowledge
increased, the precious secret became known at
length throughout the German States.   The history
of the imperial porcelain manufactory at Vienna is
one of great interest to all lovers of bric-à-brac ; and,
while mourning its decay and death, it would be
in vain to describe what difficulties were surmounted, or what efforts were made to overcome
them, in the early years of its existence.   The
foundation of this admirable manufactory bears
date only a few years later than the introduction of
porcelain into Europe ; it then produced no practical
workmen or artists ; it had no traditional theories to
improve upon ; its progress, in fact, was left entirely
to its own resources, and its sole examples were of
foreign manufacture.   Its only standard at that
period were specimens brought from China and
Japan.   Meanwhile, the public had to be won over
to the fact that examples of European ware could
equal the productions of the East in cheapness and
beauty ; for at this period Oriental china was alone
admired.   Above all, the Viennese manufacturers
had to contend with the mystery that encircled the
invention of modern china—a secret then confined

to a few individuals, who assumed the title of
"Arcanists," and who took every precaution to hide
their secret, as may be seen in any brief history of
Böttcher and Meissen. At length, however, a few
clever artists who worked at the Meissen factory
were sufficiently keen as to obtain the secret from
their employers, and these were largely bribed by
German princes to circulate their knowledge.
Artists or arcanists then contracted for various sums
for their labour ; but rarely were they induced to
sell their precious knowledge. To such causes may
be attributed the complete failure of the subsequent
manufactures of Munich, Limppenburg, &c., in the
eighteenth century, nor can it be supposed that the
Vienna establishment did not suffer from the like
causes. The actual foundation of the imperial
factory was said to be dated in the year 1718, and
at that period was the second in Europe. Some
assert that it was established by one Stenzel, a
captured arcanist from Meissen, who had been en-
ticed away by a Dutchman of the name of Claude
Innocenz de Blaquier—no doubt a very innocent
gentleman—war-agent to the imperial government.
The more correct version, however, is, that De

Blaquier himself was the actual founder; at all events this enterprising individual had been instructed by the higher powers to establish various factories in the capital; and having previously acquired some knowledge in chemistry, besides being in some measure acquainted with the composition of porcelain—which he had obtained from the writings of Jesuit missionaries in China—he set to work to ascertain if the means of its production, both as regards quality and quantity, were obtainable within the imperial territory. Having satisfactory proof on this head, he resolved to establish a manufactory, and engaged Stenzel as one of his coöperatives. With this object in view, De Blaquier proceeded secretly to Meissen, where he contrived to scrape acquaintance with that arcanist in a coffee-house. He engaged with Stenzel in a game of billiards, taking care to lose, and thus he secured his object. Stenzel, after some slight hesitation, accepted an offer of a thousand dollars to be paid yearly, together with a house rent-free, and a carriage at his disposal, and proceeded forthwith to Vienna. Subsequently De Blaquier obtained a patent for twenty-five years, granted by Charles VI., signed by his imperial majesty at Luxemburg, 27th May, 1718, from which period may be dated the actual foundation of the Vienna porcelain manufactory.

In this patent it was distinctly notified that the factory was to receive no pecuniary aid from government; but an exclusive privilege was granted for the sale of porcelain, wholesale and retail, throughout the whole empire, or similar articles to those heretofore imported from the East, Majorca, or other countries.

The patent further stipulated that the ware should consist of the highest material, and should display the most elegant and well-selected forms and colours, to which end neither labour nor expense was to be spared in the endeavour to produce patterns of original forms and fancy. This done, Blaquier entered into partnership with Heinech Zerden, a Vienna merchant named Martin Peter, and an artist, Howard Hinger. The first of these was to take the commercial duties, the latter the artistic, while De Blaquier himself was to act as a general manager. They had naturally great difficulties to contend with : the productions were not equal to the Chinese, and inferior even to those of Meissen both as regards

beauty and material, taste and decoration ; and the
sale consequently moderate. The manufactory was
therefore compelled to produce coarser articles. To
this, however, there was great opposition, as the
public, accustomed to rude earthenware and pottery,
were little inclined to pay a higher price for that
which was not more refined, and more expensive.
Meanwhile De Blaquier had other difficulties to
contend with : the arcanist, not having been regu-
larly paid according to his contract, returned to
Meissen, and not only took his secret with him, but
maliciously destroyed many of the models he had
designed. The works of the factory were consequently suspended at the end of the second year,
without a knowledge of the secret or material.
Meanwhile, being a man of great energy and deter-
mination, De Blaquier endeavoured, by numerous
experiments, to discover the genuine porcelain-
mixture ; and his efforts were finally crowned with
success, though scarcely attaining the perfection of
Meissen. His next course was that of instructing
the workmen. The factory was at first established
in a small house belonging to Count Kufstein, opposite the palace of Prince Lichtenstein, and therein

De Blaquier worked with only ten assistants and one kiln. But in the year 1721 it was removed to a house belonging to Count Breuner, where a part of the establishment remained till its close. Here the workmen were increased to twenty hands, and more kilns were erected. Nevertheless the factory was not successful; and De Blaquier, after twenty-five years' labour, decided in the year 1744 to offer it to the government. The establishment was then in good working condition, and the workmen for the most part very efficient; and he proposed to take on himself the direction and management.

At that period, however, Austria was labouring under difficulties. The, young Empress Maria Theresa looked sadly on the position of her empire. Nevertheless she resolved to support the factory, which promised to give occupation and profit to her subjects, honour and gain to the state. She therefore commanded that it should be taken by state contract from its owner, that its debt of 45,449 florins should be paid off, and De Blaquier receive the direction, with a salary of 1500 florins a-year. Thus the factory, after many difficulties and struggles, was placed on a sounder foundation. I have already

named that hitherto it had not attained the perfection of Meissen either as regards material, decoration,
taste, or invention; consequently, it was obliged to
produce cheap articles: add to this their designs
were not original,—they copied simply the works of
Japan and China very cleverly, but not in successful
rivalship as to price.   Meanwhile the Meissen work
was day by day becoming more chaste, both as
regards workmanship and modern novelty of design
and execution, and consequently not only obtained
the support of the Saxon court, but also that of the
best artists residing in Germany, and thus gained
the reputation that it has so long and deservedly
maintained; while that of Vienna followed with energetic steps, but only as an imitator.

The first productions of Vienna had no mark, and
the early works are therefore difficult to discover.
Still there are some in existence which bear the
factory's name, together with the date of the year in
which produced.   Subsequently some were marked
with a " W," which appears to be more ancient than
the first period of Berlin, which, under the director-
ship of Weggle, likewise bore the " W."   One of the
finest works of that period is a soup-tureen and dish,

which till recently was in the Convent of St. Florian in Upper Austria, made by order from the abbot of that convent, John Fördermier, who died in the year 1732; it may now be seen in the Austrian Museum recently established at Vienna. Modelling of groups and figures appears to have commenced at the period when the factory became the property of the government in 1747.

Jose Wiedermeyer, an artist who had distinguished himself as a teacher of his art, became the master modeller. Count Philip Kinsky and Count Rodolph Cholert took great interest in the development of the factory, and in 1760, under government control, it advanced rapidly to that perfection of art it subsequently maintained. Commencing with twenty labourers, they were soon doubled. The means for their payment being found by the state, and the increased sale of its productions, 24,000 florins had been made over on account. The buildings were enlarged ; new workshops and kilns were erected.

In 1751 the Princess Dowager of Lichenstein, a princess of Savoy, made over, for a trifling sum, a house adjoining the factory, on the agreement that two apprentices named by the head of that princely house should always be instructed free of charge, and during their apprenticeship supported. In 1764 the buildings were again enlarged; and in 1771 new kilns, workshops, and laboratories were also added. In fact, from the period the manufactory became government property, its progress was rapid. I have already stated that in 1750 the workmen only numbered forty; eleven years later that number had increased to one hundred and forty; and in 1761 the sale of china not only reached the sum of 50,000 florins, the factory which hitherto had been protected by the state not only supported itself, but was enabled to repay 16,000 florins of its old debt.

In the course of the sixteenth year it increased still more rapidly; and at the end of the year 1770 showed a profit of 120,000 florins, having 200 labourers, which in the year 1780 numbered 320. But this rapid increase had no solid foundation. From 1740 to 1790 was the best period for figures and groups, generally termed plastic work, while from 1780 to 1820 painting on china met with great success, the subjects being generally taken from Watteau, Laneret, and Bouchet, also allegorical representations of children, fortune and love—the latter however had little originality or taste.

When the factory became the property of the state, every article was marked with the arms of Austria, without colour—subsequently with a shield with blue cross lines ; this mark was retained till the cessation of the factory; and from the year 1784, to the third or Lörgenthal period, it was also the custom to mark every piece with the number of the year. I name this, as it may be of great assistance to the inexperienced bric-à-brac hunter, who seeks early specimens of Vienna porcelain.

On the 20th of July, 1784, the Emperor decided that the factory should be sold by auction, and although the sum fixed as a limit for the sale was not half of its real value, not an individual made an offer.

This saved the factory ; and its best period, commenced by Baron Lörgenthal, marked out an entirely new era of taste and production ; and Vienna, heretofore an imitator, acquired such powers of invention as soon to become an originator in beauty of form and design ; indeed, second to no European factory. Lörgenthal knew the great

value of artistic work ; and all his . productions
were consequently ornamental, richly decorated, but
simple and tasteful; indeed, the art was brought to
the highest perfection, while at the same time the
price was reduced as much as possible. At this
period artists and painters of the highest talent and
public reputation were employed. The preparation
of colours—a very important question in porcelain
decoration—was intrusted to a first rate chemist or
arcanist, Joseph Leithner. Under such auspices,
painting on Vienna china was not to be surpassed,
although considered, during the period to which I
allude, not equal to Sèvres or even Dresden. There
exist specimens of unrivalled beauty and consummate
taste, both as regards colour and unequalled gilding.
Indeed, I have seen cups and vases equal to, if not
surpassing, any other factory, Capo di Monte and
Bueno Retiro excepted.

Thus the Vienna porcelain manufactory, as time
passed on, having as it were gained the summit of
perfection, gradually increased in beauty as in art.
The master pieces of Raphael and Titian, Rubens
and Gerard Dow, Guido Reni and Carracci, Rem-
brandt and Claude, as also the works of living

artists, were copied with the greatest possible perfection on porcelain, coloured from the finest selections.

Leithner continued to enrich the factory by his inventions. He used the finest gold; and brought the gilding to the utmost perfection : moreover he discovered a rich cobalt blue, and a red-brown colour, which no other factory could imitate ; while his glazing was remarkably smooth. In fact, every branch of the ceramic art was improved during Lörgenthal's direction, which was naturally accompanied by an equal commercial success.

Such was the position of the factory when Lörgenthal died in 1805, after having been at the head of the establishment for 20 years.

Lörgenthal was succeeded by Niedermeyer, but war soon affected the pursuits of arts ; and in 1809, one hundred and fifty of the workmen left the factory to carry the knapsack.

Nevertheless, in 1818, its motto might most justly have been, " Aucto splendore resurgam," and when the century festival took place, notwithstanding past misfortunes and difficulties, the Imperial factory had reason to boast of its laurels ; and then employed 500 workmen.

The years from 1785 to 1815 were the most
flourishing; and the Vienna manufactory might
then be fairly considered second to none in Europe.
From 1827, however, under the direction of Scholz,
who followed Niedermeyer, it was on the decline—
economy, clay of inferior quality, indifferent workmen, copies from French models, bad artists—and
its doom was sealed. The splendid gilding, artistic
shapes, lovely groups, and exquisite painting, all
gave place to cheaper and less-refined productions; and that which heretofore might most justly
be considered a manufactory of the highest art
dwindled into a modern factory of a secondary
class. The expense to the state was therefore
great.

Sèvres, Meissen, and Berlin have, however, now
lost their formidable rival. The Vienna factory's
doom was fixed by the imperial parliament, and it
has disappeared from the circle of its younger
Austrian colleagues, for which it was once the
standard; who may profit by its history. The books
on art, and all the drawings of its most successful
period, many of its models, its library, its ceramic
collection, were given to the Austrian Museum,

recently established in Vienna, to be retained as a lasting memorial of its celebrity.

I cannot quit Vienna without recommending the bric-à-brac hunter to pay a visit to the small but admirable museum, founded from private resources and loans, since the death of the Imperial Factory; and thence to the modern factory of Herr Fischer, in Vienna. His productions, if not equal to those of the old factory, are worthy of all praise and consideration, and his courtesy and attention are admirable. There are several good and not unreasonable bric-à-brac shops in Vienna; others of a totally different nature, but in one and all a really good well-gilded specimen is unobtainable without considerable outlay.

QUEST X.

ITALY.

UNITED Italy is still a fair field for the bric-à-brac hunter, overrated as are its natural beauties and climate by the holiday traveller. Nevertheless, a few months of man's life may be passed there with considerable gratification. Rome at present I leave to the Romans. Meanwhile we have Venice, and its world-wide renown, and exquisite glass of other days, if you can get any, and highly-glazed or enamelled pottery called "Venus Porselayne," of very ancient date. Its manufactory ceased in 1822, and its productions, though interesting, were never very fine: its mark a double red anchor. Naples also once boasted a factory, named Capo di Monte, and the china there manufactured is the most rare, if really good, and most beautiful of all Italian porcelain. While in the neighbourhood of Florence, Doccia (or Genori), more ancient than Capo di Monte, had, and still has, in the days we live in one of the

largest manufactories of Europe, producing even finer
specimens than in the past. In Turin, or Vineuf
called Turin, and in Milan, as indeed in numerous
internal towns of Italy, the energetic hunter may
still discover something worthy of research.

We will first make a short *séjour* at Venice—
" that glorious city on the sea." The very writing of
the name excites the lover of art, and creates a
longing to be there. Sky, air, and water are as of
yore, but those who peopled the scene live only in
history. All the peculiarities which marked their
nationality and independence are gone. Even the
national dress, the red tabano of the men, and the
black soudale of the women, have entirely disappeared. Still Venetian interests remain, and will
for ever. Starting from Vienna, it is immaterial
which route you select, whether over the Semmerang
or the Brennen. If time be no object, the lover of
nature, no less than the lover of art, will be amply
repaid; indeed, it has ever been a matter of astonishment to me that, while autumn-holiday-seekers travel
over the beaten tracks of Europe, so few are found in
Vienna, or wandering amid the beauties of Lower
Austria : the one, as I have said, a city full of interest

and pleasant society, the other offering charms of
nature which, if rivalled elsewhere, cannot be surpassed. As regards Venice, there are probably few
who will read these pages who are not aware that
our own factory of Chelsea, whose productions rival
nearly all others in beauty of taste and decoration,
emanated from Venice ; and there is so much similarity between the best periods of Venetian and
Chelsea porcelain, that it is by no means improbable
that the same workmen were employed. Both
manufactories adopted the anchor as their mark.
Venice, or rather Murano, can boast more particularly of its exquisite glass; but although many
splendid collections still exist, good specimens, if any,
are rare in the bric-à-brac market of Europe. The
islands dotted about Venice in the Lagune have
great interest. Among them the most considerable,
and certainly the most flourishing, was Murano. It
formerly possessed the most perfect glass manufactory of Europe, not only during the Middle Ages, but
till the beginning of the last century. Mirrors and
every species of production in shape, colour, and
design were made there with immense skill and
taste. It is said that Henry III. of France, when

visiting the manufactory in 1574, ennobled the whole
of the workmen. If true, they fully deserved it. In
addition to the beauty of the Venice crystal, it was
supposed to possess the virtue of detecting poison.
The cup or glass shivered to atoms if any envenomed
beverage was poured into it—rather a valuable property this at the table of Alexander VI., or the
Duchess of Ferrara. In addition to the glass-works
the island contains a fine cathedral of the ninth
century.

Murano still holds its head above the Venetian
waters, and claims a race of men, descendants from
the old Venetian glass-workers, who have not quite
forgotten the art; nor are form, beauty, and tone of
chaste colouring quite banished from their minds.
They have worked on patiently, always hoping and
believing that Venice would some day awake from
her lethargy, and retake her position. Their hopes
are so far realised. Murano has produced a work-
man, by name Lorenzo Pladé, who has discovered, if
not precisely all, yet many of the lost secrets, while
the energy, love of art, and patriotism of Salviati
have gone far to revive the ancient splendour of
Venetian glass. And yet beautiful, very beautiful,

as are many of the modern productions, to the real
connoisseur, their date is at once evident. The old
Venetian glass was light, bright, and vitreous in
appearance, while it displayed the richest possible
colours. To a great extent all these merits are
retained in the revival at Murano. Venetian glass
is that which is commonly named blown glass; thus
every piece is an original work of human ingenuity,
and the same material is used as in the days of old.

The millefiore, the smelze, perfect imitations of
agates, lapis lazuli, the rich ruby colours, the brilliant
aventurine, some in imitation of old glass, some more
modern imitations, are to be had in London, Paris,
and elsewhere, and they are charming. Venetian
enamels have always been famous, and among the
peculiar productions of Venice may be reckoned the
beautiful composition called aventurine, the secret of
which is said to be in the possession of a single
manufacturer. As regards Venetian mirrors, once
unrivalled, they have lost much of their reputation,
as foreign competitors produce larger sheets. The
annual cost of the substances employed in the manufacture is estimated at 7,000,000f. In the East there
is a constant demand for heads and other articles,

known as conterie. There are six glass-works in
Turin, three in Genoa, five in Milan, thirteen in
Florence, eleven in Naples, and twenty in Venice;
which fifty-eight works produce articles of the
annual value of 60,276,725f. But, alas, it is only
too true, as in china, glass, jewelry, and bric-à-brac
generally, say nay who will: while science, as regards
machinery, electricity, chemistry, and every other
"istry," has advanced with rapid strides, taste, beauty,
refinement, elegance of form, outline, and colour—
art itself, in fact—have retrograded.

This was strikingly evident in the Paris Exhibition. Splendid as were the productions in modern
glass, exquisite as was much of the engraving, beautiful as the modern Wedgwood, Minton, and other
pottery, to the true lover of art they bear no possible
comparison to the works of other days. I do not say
that a vase, a cup, a group, cannot be produced to-
day as it was half a century since, true in form and
outline. I do not assert that a glass, true in texture,
graceful in form, and lovely as regards engraving,
cannot now be, and is not, made—indeed, the glass
is probably more sparkling and clear, the engraving
produced by machinery is perhaps more firm and

accurate; but it is all copied from the works of the
older times, and invariably is found wanting in that
refined grace which does not admit of imitation.
They are simply revivals. Fine art is a gift from
God, as is genius and all natural talents. A person,
in fact, may learn to draw—a school-girl may play a
sonata, after long practice, in tolerable time, not
taste; but the one would never make an artist, the
other never a musician. I have oft-times met with
women positively plain in face, though not in form
—the figure of a woman must be good, or she can
never be elegant—whose charms of manner and
grace made her far more lovely than the belle who
could boast faultless features and complexion. So it
is with high art; the work of an original genius
bears an indescribable, unknown character, that
mere manipulative skill can never attain. Let us
remember, when we bewail the degeneration of
ceramic beauty and elegance, that the leading
modellers, painters, gilders of the last century were
all artists and men of taste—men who, nevertheless,
were passing rich on five pounds a-week. To find
similar men in the present day, you must pay them
fifty, nay a hundred; and how much would a cup

and saucer, a vase, a group, a decanter, or a wine-glass cost? Why, the sum for which they are oft-times sold at Christie's; and how few are enabled to obtain them! Would Landseer, or Frederick Tayler, or such men, paint on china? and if so, what would be the value of such ceramic treasures? And yet, in other days, what exquisite groups and pas-torals after Watteau! What graceful heads of the Greuze school! No, it is too evident that modern imitative specimens may have beauty, but they lack the exquisite taste and refined art of our ancestors. And interesting and beautiful as are many of Salviati's productions, they bear no comparison, as far as art is concerned, to the finest specimens of old Venetian glass. The Murano workmen have, how-ever, much appreciation of colour, which is so abso-lutely necessary in glass-work. Moreover, their climate has a colour-brightening power, which in the glow of sunlight is rarely attained elsewhere. This warm temperature assists their art, and the tradition of the place doubtless inspires the workmen with energy to obtain future fame and profit.

Milan I have ever considered not the finest, but the most agreeable city for a brief *séjour* in the

dominions of King Victor Emmanuel. A sight of the
Duomo, as all the travelled world are aware, is worth
a journey from Venice. To the bric-à-brac hunter
Milan can also boast, or could a short time since, of
a tolerably-stocked preserve. At all events, much
interest and amusement may be derived by a day or
two spent in ransacking in the numerous curiosity-
shops. So let us leave the city of the Adriatic,
gondoliers and glass-blowers. The route, like most
others in Italy, say nay who will, possesses no great
attractions; indeed there is a tameness, or rather
sameness, in Italian scenery generally by no means
enlivening—rows and rows of mulberry and other
trees, with the vine clustering round the stems, and
trellised from tree to tree. This monotony, however,
is somewhat broken from Venice to Milan by a sight
of the strong forts which constitute the so-termed.
Quadrilateral, the beautiful lake La Guardia, and
its distant background of mountains.

On the last occasion that chance led me by this
route—the chance being the arrival of King George
of Greece at Athens, to whom I had conveyed some
possibly important communication—thence by the
Adriatic to Trieste, my good fortune offered me a

most agreeable *compagnon de voyage*, whom I soon
ascertained to be interested in the search of bric-à-
brac—a pastime, he pleasantly observed, which
ofttimes led one without knowledge into a den of
thieves, and always into some expense. "I knew a
friend, for instance," he observed, "an admirable
judge, who was constantly in the habit of saying to
his friends, 'If you ever hear of anything worth
having, drop me a line; never mind the distance, I
will go to see it. If you are confident of its merits,
and can get it at a reasonable price, buy it; I will
always give a fair percentage.' Having received a
letter on one occasion, saying that a valuable
Wedgwood vase was to be had for a mere song—this
I believe to be a usual term—he desired his servant
to pack up his carpet-bag, and started on a journey
of a hundred miles to secure it. Happily the game
was worth the playing for; but on another occasion,
on returning home, he found two very pretty vases
on his table, marked with a golden anchor, decoration, birds, and flowers—in fact, a charming pair of
vases—with the following note : 'Dear Fred, I think
I have done you good service, inasmuch as I have
secured two charming Chelsea vases, marked with

the golden anchor, and, will you believe it? they
cost only twelve pounds, which you can remit at
your convenience. The price is certainly moderate—
the vases lovely.' 'Very moderate,' exclaimed my
friend ; 'confound the fellow, I can buy them in
London for half the money. Chelsea vases, indeed !
Why, I would have given a hundred pounds for such
a pair—no disrespect to the justly celebrated English
firm which produced them, for beautiful were they ;
but the golden anchor is a bait which has hooked by
the pocket many an unwary and inexperienced bric-
à-brac hunter.'" I am not aware that Milan ever
produced any native ceramic talent, nor was there,
nor is there a porcelain factory of any great merit ;
yet specimens of Venetian glass majolica, Venice and
Naples china, and other Italian specimens, may occasionally be found. Milan, however, like all other great
cities, has been much hunted, and the coverts are not
seldom drawn blank. Much the same may be said
with reference to Turin—a pleasant city on the river
Po ; far less cheery, however, since it ceded its
dignity as the Sardinian capital to the lovely city, as
most people term Florence, on the Arno, and became
a mere city of united Italy. Vineuf, called Turin,

had formerly a fabric of some note, of hard paste china, under the direction of Gionnetti—its mark A × and a V—the cross standing for the arms of Savoy. At Turin, I have not seldom discovered some fine specimens of Wedgwood and Sèvres—how they got there I know not.

From Turin, touching at Bologna, where, as in all other Italian towns, the bric-à-brac hunter may rest a day with interest as regards the fine arts, and not always without success in his researches, let us pass by the grand mountainous railway, through innumerable tunnels, to Pistoia and Florence. There is nothing richer in all Italy than the Pistoiese, as the district round Pistoia is called, and it abounds with pleasant summer nooks, far cooler and more healthy than the sweltering baths of Lucca or Pisa, and other places where travellers do resort in crowds, solely because it is the fashion; and thence to Florence, where in summer time the sun shines with a vengeance, though the birds do not sing—(are there any birds?)—and life does not begin until the evening, when there is a burst of existence, which fairly astonishes every one that is not acquainted with Italy. The population is all abroad, lounging, and smoking—looking, and being looked at, in tight boots, kid gloves which are cheap;—of stockings I know nothing. The noise of carriages and people out so late, however, prevent all hope of sleep to those who require rest.

While in mid-winter, deny it who will, there are days and nights as cold as in the much reviled *perfide Albion*, with not a tenth of the indoor comfort; indeed, during the winter past, snow not only fell, but remained in the streets, and a sight of the snow-clad mountains in the distance is sufficient to ice a bottle of champagne, and causes human nature to cry aloud for warm clothing; and yet the invalid English leaves his native land for such places, with a far better climate, and far finer scenery within a few hours of the metropolis. Still the travelling world do boldly assert that it is impossible to imagine any object more lovely than the view of Florence from any of the heights by which the city is commanded : to enjoy these views you must get there, and I am bold enough to believe that, embracing as these views do many charms, the real lover of nature will be greatly disappointed without he chance to find himself there when the landscape

is painted with the green of early spring, or under
the auspices of some peculiar sky or atmosphere, for
the Arno can scarce be called a river, save at some
few miles beyond the city, when the country, as the
winding stream, is charming during the period when
the leaf is on the woodlands, and water most pleasing
to the eye ; moreover there are no grand trees,
and the celebrated casine, the public lounge and
resort alike of pedestrians as cavalleros, can no more
be compared to our London Parks, the Bois at
Paris, or the Prates at Vienna, than a tea garden
to the Park at Blenheim. For all that, Florence
is a pleasant abiding place, and was far more so
ere it became the capital of Italy, and was not more
expensive than Paris. To the lover of art it abounds
in interest, and the bric-à-brac hunter may find
sport ; though forsooth at Florence, as elsewhere,
little remains, save in private houses and collections,
worthy of much notice, and the price asked for
anything really worth having is fabulous; as, may I
briefly remark, is the cost of living, which is at
least trebled. There are many bric-à-brac, or curiosity shops ; perhaps the best being that of Gagliardi,
who is as well known in London as at Florence,

and of whom I can speak with the highest respect; would that I could do so of many others. A visit to the porcelain manufactory of Doccia near Florence, founded by the Marquis of Genori in 1770, offers untold pleasure to the bric-à-brac hunter. It existed previous to that of Capo di Monte at Naples, and there are still specimens of its early period, bearing the arms of Florence, and a mark apparently that of the cathedral; but they are rare and difficult to obtain. In fact, Florence can fairly boast of its production of china as far back as 1575 to 87. There are two lines of railway now open from Florence to Rome. The one by the way of Pistoia, or Pistoya, to Leghorn, Nunchetella, Civita Vecchia, to Rome; the other shorter and more direct, by Albano to the Pope's scanty dominions. The former is far the most interesting as regards scenery, as in many parts the line touches the Mediterranean, whereas the other has little to recommend it, after passing Albano; moreover, having a desire to refresh human nature by the wayside, better provide your creature comforts, or travel by night and sleep if you can, till the campagna bursts on your waking eyes, and the dome of St. Peter's welcomes you to Rome. Well do

I recollect one intensely hot night in June of the year past, when travelling with a very agreeable Englishman from Rome to Florence, who was utterly ignorant of aught but his native language, and a few words of French, that, on arriving at Viterbo, we were parched with thirst and considerably hungry. " Fifteen minutes," said the guard, opening the door. "What does he say?" exclaimed my companion, rubbing his eyes, we had previously scarcely spoken. " We remain here a quarter of an hour." "Thank God!" he replied, "do you speak the language ?" " Yes !" " Well I implore you to ascertain if we can get anything to eat, or more particularly to drink, or I shall die with hunger and thirst." In vain we sought for a buffet or refreshment room ; there was none, or if so it was closed. At length in despair we beheld an individual, who looked like a brigand, place a three-legged table on the platform, and then produce a basket, into which he dived and took therefrom some half-starved, cold roasted fowls, some hard sausages well seasoned with garlic, and some coarse bread, and sundry little basket bottles, common to Italy, containing a white wine of the country. In an instant he was surrounded by some

score of apparently half-famished and thirsty
passengers; bottles were seized on, fowls torn leg
from leg, and even the horrid sausages were rapidly
consumed as if they had been delicacies from Oxford
or Cambridge. The onslaught was gallant and soon
over; not a vestige of meat or drink remained, ere
ten minutes had elapsed, and to judge from the
pleasant grin on his brigand-looking face, the
purveyor was doubtless satisfied with his receipts,
though I doubt much if all the consumers paid their
due. In the scuffle, barring the garlicky sausages
which were consumed by the natives, we managed
to secure between us about three bottles of the
wine, which was a refreshing species of sweet cider,
and about two chickens, the size of large pigeons,
offering about as much nourishment as a piece of
dry toast—such is the gastronomic indulgence
usually found on Italian railway lines, for bric-à-brac
hunters or sight-seers, save at Bologna, where the
food is not to be complained of. Meanwhile we
returned to our carriage as satisfied as if we had
enjoyed a repast fit for Lucullus, and my subsequent friend having thanked me for my assistance,
lighted a remarkably large regalia, and throwing

himself back in the carriage, took off his coat and exclaimed, "Now for Florence. Yet I think I could drink another bottle of that wine. Is it too late to procure one ? "

Of Rome I have little to say here, all the travelled world know that a visit there offers attractions even superior to that sought by the bric-à-brac hunter. Yet it is indeed a pleasant pastime—knowing, and having again and again lingered over every portion of the ancient city—to peep once more into the various curiosity shops where in days gone by many an exquisite specimen of European porcelain have I obtained. Indeed chance, while hunting, enabled me some few years since, to discover a worthy grocer, who combined the sale of soap, sugar, and candles, with a sort of fanatic love for what he termed the "fine arts;" and so having passed through his shop, which smelt strongly of pickled herrings, garlicky sausages, oil, coffee, sugar and dips, I was one day introduced to the upper regions of his strange and somewhat dirty abode, when great indeed was my astonishment, having mounted some sixty pair of stone stairs, to find myself in a sort of lumber, indeed, two or three lumber-rooms, the

whole sides of which, from ceiling to floor, were
hung with pictures of all sorts and sizes, but no
great value; while floor and tables were covered
with every conceivable and inconceivable article of
china, of and from all nations, together with glass
and bronzes, scattered in a strange medley, dusty and
dirty, one third of which articles were broken or
cracked.   Indeed, on first entering the room I felt so
dazzled and surprised, and so full of hope that I
should be enabled to obtain some prizes, that I sat
me down for a moment calmly to contemplate the
mass of bric-à-brac, previous to its more careful
examination.

Like a scene in a play, when looked on by
daylight, however, and not from the centre of a
well-lighted house, so was the result; amid all this
heterogeneous collection, gathered together by the
grocer, there was little to attract; nevertheless I
could not but regard him with respect, considering
the combination of fine taste in a man who, thus
from pickles, contemplated pictures. Here and
there, however, I did discover a cup or two, with
marks attractive to collectors.   If so be, however,
the grocer charged for his sugar and dips in pro-

portion to the amount he expected for his bric-à-
brac, I fear his customers must have been as limited
in taste, or rich in unlimited means. At length,
however, my eyes rested on a coffee service, which I
instantly discovered to be a charming set of cream-
coloured or Queen's ware Wedgwood, with black
Egyptian characters in relief; and I am ashamed
to say immediately practised, as in such cases is per-
missible, or you will get nothing abroad, some
trifling passes of hypocrisy—call them, out of courtesy,
diplomacy—by showing an apparent indifference,
which I certainly did not feel, as to my becoming
their possessor; a bargain was, however, at length
struck, and I carried away my treasures at a very
moderate outlay. Wedgwood, however, save by
persons of real taste and judgment, or by dealers
who are perfectly alive as to its value, is not particularly estimated on the continent; in fact, foreigners
have not the taste to appreciate the most elegant of
ceramic art; were it so, the King of Prussia would
not allow very many exquisite Wedgwood vases to
remain hidden from the world, and half destroyed at
Charlottenburg. A few years since, when passing
through Rome, I lost a chance which I have ever

since regretted; this loss arose from a slight un-
certainty on my part, as to their authenticity (and a
still slighter purse), of four Capo di Monte figures, of
some size, representing the four quarters of the world.
These beautiful figures were afterwards purchased,
I am told, by Mr. Gladstone, for a much larger sum
than that for which at the time I might have secured
them, and are now, I fancy, at Kensington. In
many private houses in Rome, particularly among
the cardinals and higher priesthood, there are also
some very fine specimens of Capo di Monte and
Sèvres, and in many instances I fancy they might
be purchased for a reasonable outlay, together with
various fine specimens of Majolica and Italian
ware.

Naples is always associated in my mind with its
beautiful bay, and its ancient china manufactory of
"Capo di Monte," which, in the opening of these
pages, I named as having vanished from Italy—a
fact well known to all collectors. The famous factory of Capo di Monte was founded by Charles III.
in 1736. This beautiful ware could not have
originated from any German source ; inasmuch as,
independently of its having very little resemblance

to the productions of that country, there was scarcely time for the art to have reached Naples in so short a time after its discovery at Miessen.

Charles often worked in the manufactory with his own hands, and took great interest in its success. Starrien Porter, in a letter to Mr. Pitt (Lord Chatham), dated April 8th, 1760, speaking of that factory, says, " He is particularly fond of his china factory at Capo di Monte." During the fairs held annually in the square before the Palace at Naples, there is a shop or stall solely for the sale of his china, and a note was matutinally brought to the King of the articles sold, together with the names of the purchasers, on whom he looked favourably. On obtaining the Crown of Spain, he took with him twenty-two persons to form his establishment at Madrid, one of whom, ninety-five years of age, was living in Naples in 1844.

Private factories were subsequently formed at Naples, where many of the models, gold and other articles, used in the Capo factory, were stolen; and they all closed in 1821.

In the royal establishment—*Alla Vita della Sanità* — many valuable specimens may still be

seen, which will greatly interest the bric-à-brac
hunter.

Au reste, save at particular periods and seasons,
Naples itself has few charms. I do recollect, however, one memorable evening at the latter end of
August, sitting with a kind friend on the balcony of
our hotel on the Chiaja, having witnessed the glorious
sun sink behind Posilipo, and then, as the deep red
air of twilight became deeper in its glow, the full
moon rose from the far mountains of the Sorrentine
shore, over bay, and blue isle, and clear promontory,
and glassy sea, filling the measure of nature's beauty
to the brim, and certainly causing me to feel at the
moment that a bright moonlight night of early
autumn, over the Bay of Naples, was unrivalled,
and in its short existence it probably is so. I
mention this trifling fact, inasmuch as travellers for
the most part invariably speak of places, or generally
so, from the impression left on their minds at the
moment, or during a cursory visit, and had I left
Naples on the morning subsequent to that delicious
night I should certainly have considered the city and
its bay, with its setting sun and rising moon, the
most charming spot in Europe. But I have chanced

to see the bay when it was anything but calm or agreeable, and have looked on the gardens of the Villa Real when they were cold, and cheerless, and leafless ; and although for the most part there is an aspect of vivid animal existence, a brightness, a life, a cheerfulness, about the city, there exists at the same time a confusion, disorder, filth, foul smells, and ill drainage, which go far to annul the romantic impressions, caused by a sight of Vesuvius, the distant Capri, surrounding beauties, and charming environs. In fact, Naples has many charms; but a residence there, save it be a brief one, will chase them away.

Numerous as are the bric-à-brac shops at Naples, chance nevertheless will there obtain for you anything worth having, though doubtless there, as at Rome and elsewhere, there are treasures in private houses which scarcely ever see the light of day, and the value of which is scarce known to their owners. I had once the very good fortune to obtain two most exquisite Venetian glasses, of rich ruby colour, and many-coloured flowered stems ; these I entrusted to a packer, who assured me the box which contained them might be thrown from the top of Fort Angelo

without fear of breakage; nevertheless they reached
England in a hundred pieces, so beware of Neapolitan
packing. In proof of their beauty, I was offered
money for the remnants.

Majolica, or as it is commonly called, Faenza or
Raphael ware, is a fine enamelled earthenware of
the end of the fifteenth century, and the early part
of the sixteenth century. This pottery may be
found in more or less beauty and artistic taste in
almost every European museum and collection, and
much of an inferior kind can still be purchased in
all Italian cities as elsewhere. For my own part, I
admit no great love for this species of ceramic art,
though many of the productions are replete with
beauty, artistic powers, and originality. The original
title of majolica, so say many authors, is supposed to
have been derived from Majorca, because it greatly
resembles, and was probably founded on the Moorish
pottery and enamelled dishes brought from Majorca
by the Pisans in the twelfth century, and afterwards by other trading cities along the coast.
Whether it originated at Majorca or not is, however,
of little importance to those collectors who seek it,
and are capable of judging of its beauty and early

authenticity, inasmuch as in the present day, in
Italy, particularly at Doccia, in France also, ay,
and by our own celebrated Minton, it is imitated
with great beauty aud artistic taste, and in some
cases so truly as to defy the knowledge of the
best judges.   As regards Majorca being its birth-
place, I have seen among the *canards*, during the
trial of the brave and murdered Admiral Byng—
whom I feel pride in claiming as an ancestor—that
his great love for this ware and other ceramic
treasures having caused him to visit the residence
of some person in that island who possessed a rare
specimen, and with whom he was bargaining for the
possession, when a messenger arrived to inform him
the French fleet was in the offing, turning to the
messenger, he replied, " Look here, this rare specimen is worth all the French fleet ; tell Captain ——
to prepare for action, and the French to wait till I
have secured it."   Although it is probable that the
term majolica was derived from Majorca, there does
not appear to be any authentic evidence of this fact ;
on the contrary, it appears first to have been made
at Faenza, where it was principally made or exported, while some French antiquaries. claim a still

greater age for the French term, Fayence, and insist
that it was derived from Fayenne, an obscure town
in France, where there is said to have been a pottery
long before it existed at Faenza in Italy.   Mr. Bohn,
in his very useful work, a guide to ceramic.knowledge,
particularly to inexperienced bric-à-brac hunters,
tells us that during the great majolica period, it
was the fashion for lovers to present their mistresses,
or their betrothed, with small ornamental pieces
called *amatoriæ*—generally plates, dishes, or vases,
adorned with the portrait and christian name of their
favoured fair; many of these may still be seen in
various bric-à-brac shops.   They are, however, of no
great beauty or value, and certainly, as far as I have
seen them, do not prove the taste or beauty of the
era.   However, the gift of some such majolica dishes
or vases, as I have had the good fortune to behold,
would indeed be as costly as the choicest diamond
bracelet, and though majolica, or any glazed or
enamelled pottery, may not be so pleasing to the eye,
as Sèvres, Dresden, Wedgwood, or Chelsea, it is
nevertheless of great value if good, and deeply
interesting to the collector.

   While in Italy, particularly at Florence, the bric-à-brac hunter cannot do better than take a trip to Leghorn; it is but a railway flight of two hours through some charming country, with the Mediterranean at the end of it. Not that it boasts of a porcelain manufactory, or am I aware that it ever claimed one. But there lives in that maritime town, the Chevalier Audrea Campasini, a man of genius and repute, who, with his own hand, after fourteen years of labour, produced a large and beautiful model in ivory of St. Peter's, which was not only seen by Her Majesty of England, but by half the crowned heads and artistic Societies in Europe, and from whom he received the highest testimonials.

As was his father before him, so is the Chevalier an artist and a man of taste, and he has gathered around him an inconceivable quantity of bric-à-brac, filling many rooms, which he is perfectly ready to show to anyone, and equally ready to sell. Among this heterogeneous mass, he has many good specimens, and I must admit that his demands are not exorbitant. For the benefit of those who desire to visit his collection, I may name that his residence is, Via San Francesco, 33.

In these days when everyone travels, a visit to

Copenhagen will not be an unpleasant trip to the bric-à-brac hunter—not that he will find a great selection. The old china, however, from the Royal manufactory, marked in blue, with three wavy lines which indicate the Sound, and two Belts, if a good specimen can be found, is remarkably fine and interesting. Lord Nelson was very partial to this china, and in 1801 paid many visits to the factory and purchased largely. In addition to a china hunt, a visit to the late battle fields, and the pleasant neighbourhood of Copenhagen, will well repay the trouble, while the city itself is full of interest.

QUEST XI.

PARIS.—LONDON.

WE are now in Paris, for a brief *séjour*—then to the great Babylon, and I have done. I need say but a few words as regards either city in connection with bric-à-brac. All the English world, I take it, who are unacquainted with the beautiful Imperial city, for a beautiful city it is, and day by day becomes more so, had better cross the Channel and judge for themselves. A few things are wanting; a thorough knowledge of the language, a good purse, calm temper, and a courteous manner. With these acquisitions for a brief stay, Paris as a Capital has no rival. A knowledge of the language is not only desirable, but utterly necessary for real enjoyment. Not such a knowledge as most people imagine they have who say they speak French, and who wishing for green gages, ask for " Gages Verts," and being corrected, say, What, do you call them " rainy clouds ? " —which is a fact. Money is wanted, because the

price of the necessaries of life is enhanced even to
the charging of twelve francs for an ordinary duck
or fowl; temper, because no Frenchman, save he be
a French gentleman, allows you to have the slightest
opinion of your own, even in the purchase of a pair
of gloves; and courtesy, inasmuch a sa calm, courteous demeanour in the long run subdues the inso-
lence even of a human bear.

One of the principal reasons I take it, for the
Capital of the French Empire, increasing in embel-
lishment, cleanliness, and cheerfulness, made doubly
so by the verdure of trees in all its streets and
Boulevards, during the summer, is simply, that to a
Frenchman Paris is his world, a real earthly Paradise,
his home, his mistress, his adoration; he goes to the
seaside, "les Eaux" in due season, because not to go
is to be nobody.   It is the fashion, and here, as elsewhere, that odious and undefinable word carries the
day; but he is as wretched at "les Eaux" as a lover
who is absent from her he loves, and is never happy
till he returns to the mistress of his heart, called
Paris.   London is quite another city, grand, magnificent in wealth and man's labour.   Her parks, the
most splendid in the world, women, horses and

equipages, men if you will it, when, assembled during what is termed the season, immensely superior to all beyond the Channel, which divides us from the Continent of Europe. But London, to all save those who are actually engaged in business, is a mere *séjour* of pleasure, or of fashion—fashion again—or temporary habits. There are not, I am satisfied, many thousands, in that city of millions, who do not yearn to fly to the green fields, parks, and pleasures of the country in midsummer time, and the sports, home comforts of a country house, and enjoyments of a family circle in mid-winter. Thus for all they care Leicester Square might remain a mud pond, or any other square be a courtyard; being there they like to see the Parks bright and well filled, the streets bustling and well lighted, the shops gay; but it is not their world or their Paradise. That is found only in the home circle, whether in a castle in the centre of a noble park, such as England can only show in perfection, or equally so in a rose or honeysuckle covered cottage, far from the smoke of the city, or the turmoil of money gainings and money losing. As regards bric-à-brac, Paris, as London, and I speak of them

o

together, abounds.   There are many, very many,
highly respectable and rich administrators to the
public taste as regards ceramic excellence, and bric-
à-brac as an "olla podrida." For the most part,
dealers in bric-à-brac are children of Israel, and I am
bound to believe, and do believe, that although many
have commenced the trade with very limited means
and slight experience, the constant search for beauty
in art and knowledge, gained from day to day by
experience and, if you will, love of gain—all fair in
trade—has at length caused them so to love the
pursuit, that a seller of bric-à-brac becomes sooner
or later to love his profession, and his eye and taste
enable him to acquire a thorough knowledge and
discrimination of the value of the highest and lowest
works of art.

In my rambles during many years throughout the
length and breadth of Europe, I have known men,
who, when I first visited their collections, were of
the humblest order, in a few years become indepen-
dent, nay wealthy; this may be accounted for, in
the first place, that the love for collecting the fine
arts has become notorious, and secondly, that what
was formerly purchased for a song, is now sold for

10*l.*, with tenfold the buyers. Thus, amid the numerous shops in Paris filled with bric-à-brac,—good,
bad, and indifferent,—nothing is now to be had cheap.
The man who has great knowledge may occasionally pick up something, at a fair but full value, all
others pay more or less twice that for which it might
formerly have been obtained. In Paris, as indeed
in all the small cities and towns in France, the rage
for bric-à-brac is a *furor.* Only recently I visited
the curious, but dull old town of Abbeville, where
there are two or three small bric-à-brac shops; in
both I selected one or two trifles, the sum asked for
which was most exorbitant, and yet they sell.
There is nothing good, bad, or indifferent to be had
in Paris, save for a large outlay, and as for Sèvres,
if it is even tolerable, it is estimated as bullion. In
London, as in Paris, there are crowds of bric-à-brac
dealers, good, bad, and indifferent; all that is really
good, however, in London deservedly commands high
prices, and obtains them; ordinary, but by no means
to be despised specimens, are far cheaper than
abroad, and among the first class dealers, I must do
them the justice to say, a novice may purchase
without fear. I have abstained from naming any

dealers, because I neither desire to praise, nor give offence. Again and again it has been asserted to me by London dealers, that France comes over to purchase; in like manner France asserts in language, which courtesy dare not contradict, that England acts in like manner; all I can assert is that, speaking from my own experience, if England does purchase in France, and gives a third of the price asked, the profit made must be *nil.* I am aware that first-rate dealers do come to Paris, and do advertise that they are coming with money in their pockets, and are ready to purchase ; and I conclude they are thoroughly aware of the effects of such advertisements, and it pays, or they would not risk the outlay of a journey and Paris expenses; but to an amateur collector, without he is determined to have this or that object, regardless of expense, Paris is not his market.

Previous to the advent of railways, when continental travellers were as one to fifty, when rich men travelled for pleasure, and employés were well paid for their wanderings, much might be found by the experienced collector and purchased fairly, sometimes luckily ; but that period is over, and, in those days, I conclude dealers were more or less dependent on home sales, or those who brought wares to them for purchase. Now there is scarcely a first-rate dealer who does not go or send all over Europe, regardless of expense ; they are to be met with, go where you will, at Petersburg and Moscow, Constantinople and Rome ; so I conclude it must pay. That it does so, however, is solely because the value of bric-à-brac is quadrupled. In London the valuable sales at Christy's, Phillips', and other first class auctions are constant, and generally it is wonderful the prices obtained during the season, for even moderate works of art.

In like manner at Paris, almost daily sales take place in the Rue Drouet, where every species of bric-à-brac is offered for sale—pictures of value, and mere daubs by hundreds; old and modern furniture, china, glass, in fact everything coming under the denomination of bric-à-brac, as of household goods. An occasional visit to these sales is highly amusing, even to those not afflicted with the mania of bric-à-brac hunting. Yet I must confess it is difficult for anyone having a decent coat on his back to purchase anything cheaply. There appears in fact to be a combination among dealers,

high and low, men and women, which utterly upsets
the hopes and expectations of an amateur. However,
there must be some freemasonry among them; as I
have witnesssd the selling of a piece of china to a
dealer, which I have subsequently purchased in his
shop at a less price than that he paid for it at the
sales; and I cannot but believe, that a small capital
and much knowledge of the ceramic art, will soon
convert the small into large; moreover, the knowledge is always on the increase, however few there
may be who absolutely ever attain to the perfect
acquirements of a connoisseur. During the many
years it has been my pleasure to search in every
capital and town, in which I may chance to find
myself, for bric-à-brac dealers, whether at home or
abroad, I have had practical proof of the above
assertion; for I have known men who apparently,
not ten years lang syne, were in the lowest possible
position, bordering on apparent poverty; in that
brief space become rich. In fact their history may
be written in the following lines :—

"Autrefois j'étais villageois :
On peut s'en souvenir :
Un peu sauvage, un peu sournois,
Pensant à l'avenir—

Pour te conter mes aventures,
Il faudrait peu de mots,
J'ai maintenant quatre voitures,
Au lieu de deux sabots."

Of course I do not include the higher, and well-known class of dealers, though who dare say that they have not had their early struggles ? As an illustration, however, of the rapid rise in the fortunes of those to whom I more particularly allude,—I perfectly recollect one fine summer's evening—when enjoying the *al fresco* in company with some ladies, and listening to the charming music ofttimes heard in the public gardens, within a circuit of a few miles round Vienna—being accosted by a well-dressed gentleman, gloved, hatted, and booted to perfection, who, having bowed, offered me his hand; meanwhile, having been introduced to very many agreeable foreigners, whose names are at times difficult to catch, and whose faces are still more difficult to remember, I arose from my seat, returned his bow most politely, as the pressure of his hand, and agreed with his assertion that the weather was delightful; another bow, and he walked on with a companion, while I resumed my seat. "Who is your friend ?"

inquired the lady by my side; for the moment I
could scarcely recollect, and replied, " I rather think
he is the Swedish Minister;" on taking another look
at my friend, however, as he sauntered slowly on, memory came to my aid, and I said to myself,—it cannot
be—in those kid gloves and polished boots, and yet
forsooth it is—and I burst into laughter. "What's
the joke, Colonello ?" exclaimed an agreeable young
attaché, who came up at the moment. "Joke," I
replied, "why I have just been courteously recognised
by a gentleman in lavender kids and polished boots—
whom I fancied was the Swedish Minister—and
have discovered my error in the person of H—rr.
You may recollect that last year we visited him in a
garret, the odour of which was not agreeable, the
more so as he sat in his shirt-sleeves—weather very
hot—before a horrid mess of sausage, and black
bread, of which he urged us to partake: but we
could do nothing with him as regards buying bric-à-
brac; his prices were enormous." This person, I am
credibly informed, was a servant in an Austrian
family, and came to Vienna with probably ten florins
in his pocket. I admire his energy and genius in so
speedily picking up a certain knowledge of ceramic

art—however I may dislike his manners as his dealings. "Confound him," said the *attaché*, "I met him not long since on the Präter, when he patted me on the back, asked me why I had not been to see him, and requested my photo for his album of European celebrities, for which in future days he hoped to obtain a large price. No wonder he turns out so well, when he buys for a pound and sells for ten, and gets it, though I have always marvelled who gives it—but they do give it. And what is most offensive, he is always ready to guarantee everything on oath, when dealing with men who possibly have ten times his experience and knowledge; moreover, should you presume to have an opinion of your own, or examine a mark, or ask for a magnifying-glass, he appears greatly offended. Such indeed is the system pursued by the lower class of continental dealers generally—a modern piece of china is of the last century—a cup known by a connoisseur to have issued but yesterday from a Fabric, is old Vienna, Berlin, or Dresden; a piece of Ginori which bears its own merits, and they are great, is always converted and guaranteed .by oath, for Capo di Monte. Alas! for the inexperienced

and unwary—what a fine collection they must possess!
It puts me in mind of a very old story—of fresh
fish—which is worth repeating, however ofttimes
told—I fancy ; " and throwing away his cigar, he sat
down with our party. "My tale," he added, "is
brief and simple. A gentleman sent his negro servant for some fresh fish. On arriving at the fishmonger's, and handling the fish, blacky began to smell
it.   On which the fishmonger exclaimed, ' Hallo ! you
black rascal, what do you smell my fish for.'   ' Me
no smell your fish,' the negro replied.   ' What are
you doing with it then ? '   ' Why, me talk to him,
massa.'   ' And what do you say to him ? '   ' Me
ask him what news of the sea, dat's all, and he says
he don't know, he been here dese three weeks.'"
And so it is with many a china cup, said to have
been in the same family for years, they were made
but yesterday in one Fabric, painted in another, and
marked and reglazed in another—for the market—
in which they have been only for three weeks ; but
they are far fresher than the fish. Again, I well
recollect coveting a Venice glass—being the possessor
of its fellow—which I had seen in the window of a
dealer in Italy ; having offered the price I considered

its fair value, about the third of that demanded, it was refused ; being, however, anxious to obtain the glass, I called again and added five francs to my previous offer; this was also refused. While talking with the dealer, however, a most respectably dressed woman, with evident marks of sorrow on her pale face, entered the shop, and tendered for sale a very pretty china vase, for which she solicited ten francs— about a third of its value. "No," said the dealer, "I will give you eight." "Nine," replied the poor woman in distress, "and it is yours." "Eight," again repeated the dealer, "I will give no more." On this, observing the anxiety depicted on her countenance, I interfered by saying, "I will take it, madam ; here are the ten francs"—fully intending to beg her re-acceptance of the china and the money. On which the worthy dealer became irate, and declared that I had no right to interfere with his business. "None whatever," I replied, "but inasmuch as you refused to give ten francs, I was perfectly justified in so doing— however, you are quite welcome to the bargain." He thereon paid the ten francs, and the poor woman left the shop, thanking me with tears in her eyes. As soon as she had departed, I turned to the dealer,

and said, "You expressed yourself somewhat rudely
as to my interference in your affairs. I certainly
had no intention to do so, though you are well aware
you were driving a cruel bargain with a fellow-
creature in distress. In proof of my words I will
give you fifteen francs for what you have just given
ten for," an offer he very rudely refused, and I quit-
ted his shop. Literally only two hours after, I had
occasion to visit a money-changer's, who also dealt
occasionally in bric-à-brac. On my entering his room,
he said, "I have got something which I think may
suit you." On my asking him to produce it, behold
the very vase which I had recently seen. "What do
you want for it?" "Twenty-five francs, I gave
twenty." "It is well worth it," I replied, "and more;"
and then I told him the little historiette which I
have here written, not that it has much point, but as
a simple evidence of how fortunes are commenced by
the humbler class of bric-à-brac sellers—and how
money is paid by the inexperienced hunter for articles
of little value. A thousand such dealings are of
daily occurrence, and ofttimes a prize is obtained
from misery or want, for a pound or two—not in the
most honest manner—which, as years pass, is sold

for a hundred; indeed it is well known that a rich buyer, determined to possess any object on which he has set his heart, or if determined from some particular fancy to possess, will, at a sale, run up the price of a moderate specimen to treble its actual value. Whereas a seller, who has capital and can await time or opportunity, will, in like manner, not seldom obtain far more. I would beg to remark, that I do not mention these facts with the slightest intention or desire to injure a class who have oft-times afforded me great interest and amusement, and from whose ignorance I have at times not un-fairly benefited, and from whom in the early days of my hunting, I have learnt many a valuable lesson. Moreover, it is said that in love, as in war, all things are fair within the bounds of diplomacy, to call it by the most courteous name; so are they, I fancy, in bric-à-brac markets, though the limit may be some-what larger. As, however, the object of this little book is to offer the moderate experience I possess to those whose love for ceramic art may induce them to follow in my footsteps, it is well I should, as far as may be, guard them against the difficulties and chicaneries, they will encounter in their researches.

I cannot leave the hunting grounds wherein I have passed so many days and hours of interest, instruction, and delight, and which I hope to revive, without one word to those who may have these pleasures to come. Kind nature is the mistress of all art, and it is amid scenes of beauty, created by God, as in cities, that one learns to appreciate alike His manifold gifts, as the ingenuity and refined art of man. Bric-à-brac hunting, believe me, to a collector, is a most agreeable, instructive, and innocent pursuit, wherein much is found alike to gratify the mind as the eye—till at length it becomes an engrossing passion. I may justly add—that the traveller who seeks such pursuit when wandering in foreign cities, not only learns the history of the land in which he lingers, but mentally peoples it with those who lived and loved in ages past. He becomes in fact so energetic in his pursuits as to banish all others of a less refined nature from his heart. How many are there now living, ere the advent of railways caused the facility of travel, or directors of continental excursions were born, at least as speculators, but must look back with regret to those pleasant days when few English people ever found many real travellers beyond Paris, or the now beaten tracks of Switzerland and Italy.

Petersburg, Constantinople, Berlin, Vienna, and Madrid, were then all but unknown, save to diplomatists or resident merchants. The rich and real traveller, who wheeled it through Europe in a comfortable carriage, stopped at comfortable hotels, and halted here and there by the wayside, to delight calmly in the beauties of nature and the pleasures of art. In those days there were a vast number of admirable specimens of European china and bric-à-brac to be had, worthy of being exported to the collector's emporium, at a very moderate outlay. That golden era is now for ever dead and buried. Could the man who lived a hundred years since rise from his grave, and glide, as travellers do now glide, smoothly and rapidly over Mont Cenis in a railway, I take it, when comparing the present with the past, he would jump from the window, or return to his home a lunatic. The advantage to civilization which has thus been insured by the annihilation of distance and the gain of time, who dare deny? But with all its advantages, it is not without its evils; people no longer travel by hundreds to see and learn, but rush by tens of thousands throughout Europe, without seeing much, and learning less, for the most part without knowledge of the language of the people among whom they briefly sojourn. Ofttimes, indeed, have I met with an American traveller—ay, an Englishman also—who has boasted of the short time in which he has done Europe and the East: his travel having the sole advantage of enabling him to tell his friends at home that he has been here and there, and everywhere, seen this and seen that, crossed the Mont Cenis and the Simplon, seen the Pope and Napoleon, kissed St. Peter's toe, which he had no right to kiss, and drunk no end of stuff called champagne, spent no end of money, and brought home no end of vile trash as works of foreign art. "I calculate," says an American, "I've whipped the world as to the time in which I did Europe;" while an Englishman calmly boasts that he has seen more and spent more in a six weeks' holiday than many do in a year. Thus, a respectable dealer in the various necessaries of life, in the west of London, rises one morning, and says to his wife while discussing the matutinal meal, "I have had a good season, September has arrived, we will give

Jemima a treat." He rushes to his banker, draws
for a hundred, which he intends to spend, and is off
to Boulogne, Paris, probably Switzerland, and home
again, without his hundred, or one single advantage,
save that Jemima has seen "La belle France"
through a railway window, and purchased a hideous
head-piece called a bonnet, and has paid for it double
the price for which she could have obtained a far
prettier one in London. And so with all else, in
these civilised and enlightened days, on the Continent. In good faith they are enlightened in acts
and words, which courtesy compels me to omit.
True, one travels faster and cheaper, as regards
railway fares ; in all else the expense of travelling is
quadrupled, with a tenth of its pleasures and advantages. Are there not many still living who well
recollect, when entering an English roadside hotel,
or in any county town of repute, the comfort and
cleanliness within, and fair dealing by which they
were surrounded ? Have they forgotten the rounds
of beef, the pigeon pies, the hams, the cold fowls,
which greeted them as they entered the hostelry?
Have travellers on the Continent forgotten, even
twenty years back, in France particularly, the ad-

P

mirable table-d'hôte, at three francs or half-a-crown a-head, a decent light claret included; the excellent matutinal *café au lait*, the thanks of the garçon, or waiter, on the receipt of a franc? Surely they must do so, when paying to-day half-a-crown for the wing of a chicken, and the same price for washing hands, which I positively did at a Bruxelles hotel. What have we now as regards travelling? In old England, miserable railway buffets; ay, even there, at least at the London stations, you may eat and drink, and be merry, at about one-half what you may on the Continent, and I have had a tolerable experience. Indeed, throughout Italy and Germany, you are not only pillaged in every possible manner, but half starved. I speak for the most part when *en route;* as at Vienna, Berlin, and Dresden there is still to be found comfort and comparative economy, if you judge fit to practise it; but once beyond the limits of the necessaries of life, and extras are ruinous. All these evils are naturally much against the bric-à-brac hunter; thousands buy Dresden vases, cups, &c., made yesterday, paying for them the value of real works of art. Cart-loads of bric-à-brac have recently gone to America, for the most part of no great beauty or value, the sum paid for which would set up a bank. And the lighter expense and rapidity of railway travelling, together with speedy communication by telegraph and post, enable the London and Paris dealers to send over their emissaries at a moment's notice, when apprised of a sale, or a chance of picking up anything which remains worth having. Nevertheless, to those who really love art, how much and how beautiful is there still to be seen, if not purchased, in European cities ; while the experienced and energetic hunter may still pick up something worthy his labour and research.

And now for the present I will say, readers, farewell, with the following trifling anecdote. A publisher and a wine-merchant, when in company with friends, were discussing which would make the most out of an original work. After various proofs adduced on both sides, a wager being made, it was given in favour of the wine merchant, as the publisher confessed, that however transmogrified, he was compelled to retain much of the original ; while the wine merchant confessed, that from a pipe of genuine port at last he left nothing.

I trust my publisher will be so far in the position

of the wine merchant, that however he may transmogrify, he will not have a volume of "Bric-à-brac Huŋting" remaining, at this period of the year, when the world at home cross the channel for foreign travel, whether bric-à-brac hunters or not.

THE END.

BRADBURY, EVANS, AND CO., PRINTERS, WHITEFRIARS.